The Rose Petal Floor

Erik B. Fuentes

ISBN: 150323360X
ISBN 13: 9781503233607
Library of Congress Control Number: 2014920950
CreateSpace Independent Publishing Platform
North Charleston, South Carolina

CHAPTER 1

Hang

*Z*ac, Derek, and Adan enter the Blue Soul, ready for some cocktails after their experience at the Thumping Nightclub.

"This is a different club," Derek states, looking around.

"Yeah, this is a little more chill than that crap we were stuck in," Adan says. "What is it with clubs like that? Who thinks that repetitive butt-thumping music is any good?"

"You can't hear shit. Can't talk to a woman," Zac complains.

Derek scans the room, and on his left he spots a dance floor with a stage behind it and tables in front of it. In front of them is a bar parallel to the entrance and street.

The other two follow Derek's gaze, thinking the place is cool with a subdued atmosphere and noting the music is what their parents listened to.

They take some bar chairs as Thomas, the bartender and owner, asks, "What can I get you guys?"

"How about some martinis? You guys good with that?" Zac asks.

"Yeah, I'm good," Adan replies.

"I'll have a Manhattan," Derek says, and Adan and Zac shake their heads.

"That last place sucked," Adan says when Thomas sets his martini in front of him. "Women in stretch pants and high heels. Are dresses out now? You know, what the fuck is up with women and shoes these days? They run in these six-inch heels with open toes, but their toes hang over the front of the shoe. It's like they have hang toe. Yeah, that's it, hang toe. What the fuck is that?" He questions his friends, agitated.

"There really is nothing attractive about it," Zac answers. "Do they really think it looks good? I mean, how do they not scrape their toenails or end up with toe cuts? It disturbs me. Makes me want to take them shopping."

Thomas delivers Zac's drink with a questioning look.

"What happened to classy?" Adan asks. "It all seems to be trashy fads these days. Crappy music, ugly clothes, and hang toe. What a mess."

"I kind of like the toe thing," Derek says insecurely and then takes a sip of his Manhattan.

"What? It doesn't even look good on strippers," Adan responds. "Why can't they just buy bigger shoes? Who are they kidding? If the shoe fits, you know. Well, it doesn't fucking fit, so get shoes that do." Agitated, Adan chooses to stand at the bar.

Zac and Thomas start laughing, clearly amused at the fact that Derek likes the toe thing and Adan despises it. Thomas retreats to a group of women who just arrived.

Derek remains silent, afraid of further remarks.

"Look around. The women here are in dresses and classy pumps, much better—a little class," Zac says, looking around.

The three scope the place, noticing a decisive difference with this crowd at the Blue Soul versus the Thumping Club.

"Over there." Adan points to his left.

"What? Where?" Derek replies, desperately wondering who Adan is referring to.

"Those two over there at the far corner are looking our way," an excited Adan confirms.

Zac just looks and nods his head with approval.

"I get the blonde," Derek says quickly.

"Let's get a table," Zac says, thinking they may get the women's attention if they move a little closer. The three meander to a table, keeping a couple tables between the two women and them.

The blonde and brunette notice the guys moving toward a table.

"Look at that guy," Allison, the blonde, tells Mary Ann, referring to Derek.

"Yeah, my god, he is such a looker," Mary Ann replies. "Tall, cheekbones, strong jaw, eyes. Wait, they are grabbing a table."

"I think I am going to ovulate," Allison says, sighing.

"Going to get knocked up are you?" Mary Ann continues the banter. "There are three of them, so let's wait and see." She relaxes in her chair.

"You're right. I'll calm down." Flustered, Allison sits back in her chair also, but her gaze remains on Derek.

"Those two are checking us pretty hard," Adan tells Zac.

"Yeah, that brunette is so cute," Zac responds, creating his plan of attack.

"I am going to buy that woman a drink," Derek says, referring to the blonde.

"OK," Zac immediately says, cutting off Adan before further conversation.

Derek waves to a waitress, catching her attention. "I would like to buy that blonde a drink. Would you please send over whatever she is drinking?" he asks the waitress.

"What about the other woman?" she asks.

"No, thank you," Derek says, looking at the blonde.

"Classy," the waitress says sarcastically.

"Send her friend one on me." Zac saves the situation.

Adan sits back, thinking Derek will fuck it up anyway so no need for intervention.

Delivering the cocktail to Allison, the waitress says, "This drink is from the tall gentleman over there." She points to Derek. "And this is from the gentleman next to him," she says to Mary Ann.

"Thank you," they both reply.

"Now what?" Mary Ann asks Allison.

"In a few minutes, should we go over?" Allison asks nervously.

"OK, but what about the other guy?" Mary Ann asks.

"What about him? He didn't buy us drinks did he?"

"OK."

Some '80's music plays and some patrons dance. Both tables' occupants continue to spy on each other, and Derek grows uncomfortable. He sits silently, wondering if he should approach the women or if he they're ignoring him now that they accepted the cocktails.

Adan notices Derek's anxiety and prefers to let it continue by saying nothing.

Zac remains calm and confident, watching the dancing and finding he likes this music. He notices movement from the women's table.

"OK, it's time," Allison informs Mary Ann. They both rise from their seats and pace themselves to the men's table. Both are wearing knee-length dresses. Mary Ann walks confidently in classic three-inch blue-black pumps that match her black dress, while Allison wears open-toe sling-backs, without the hang toe, and a strapless green dress.

"Hi. Thank you for the drink." Allison focuses on Derek, who is nervous and quiet for the moment.

"Thank you." Mary Ann looks at Zac, holding up her martini.

"Would you care to join us?" Zac asks the two as he reaches for chairs from another table.

"Yes," Allison blurts while Mary Ann agrees politely. They take the offered seats, Allison sitting next to Derek and Mary Ann between Allison and Zac. Adan sits across from them.

Zac introduces Derek, Adan, and himself.

"I am Mary Ann, and this is Allison," Mary Ann politely replies.

Though a stunning-looking man, Derek is insecure and quite inept with women. He leans toward Adan. "What do I do?" he whispers while Zac chats with Mary Ann and Allison.

"You know, talking to her would work," Adan suggests sardonically.

While he's whispering with Adan, Derek feels Allison place her hand on his thigh. This increases his nervous tension but bolsters his limited confidence, as he does not need to make the first move.

He leans toward Allison, and they begin some nervous small talk as the cocktail waitress arrives, asking about another round. Adan suggests more cocktails, while Zac and Mary Ann watch Derek and Allison's quirky engagements.

"Sure, I will have another martini. What would you like?" Zac asks Mary Ann.

"That sound good—I will have one also," she tells the waitress.

Adan orders another martini, while Derek asks Allison what she would prefer.

"I am drinking whiskey sours."

Derek orders another Manhattan, thinking it will boost his confidence further.

Mary Ann leans to Zac and informs him of Derek's "woman's" drink and Allison's "man's" drink. Zac laughs.

Allison continues flirting with Derek, while Zac and Mary Ann become more acquainted. After a couple more cocktails comes Derek's revelation. He picks up his phone and begins dialing.

"What are you doing?" Adan asks the question on everyone's mind.

"I am calling my mother to inform her Allison is coming for dinner tomorrow night."

Shocked and stunned, Allison pulls away from Derek. They've done a lot of flirting, but had no discussion of this.

Adan leans into Derek. "Don't you think this is a little early for that? You haven't even kissed yet. Maybe you should be a little more suggestive."

"Oh, OK. A little too soon, huh?" He returns his attention to Allison.

"I am not going to your mother's for dinner tomorrow," she says sternly.

"OK, OK, I get it. Perhaps we could get out of here?" he asks Allison suggestively, just as Adan recommended.

"What do you have in mind?" she asks as she tilts her head, with her tongue exposed in the corner of her mouth slightly.

"I was thinking we could go back to my place. I would like to slowly remove your clothes," Derek says, thinking he is finally becoming seductive.

"Then?" she asks with a sexy smile, rubbing her pinkie finger around the rim of her glass.

"Then I would like to lick and suck your nipples until you lactate," he says ever so seriously.

"What the fuck? Mommy issues with you, motherfucker? First dinner with Mommy, then you want me to lactate. You're a fucking idiot. Next time, just don't speak, and you might get laid, dumb ass." She assaults him verbally, as she feels she just was.

Allison jumps up, grabs her chair, and takes it to the other side of the table next to Adan. "Do you mind?" she asks Adan.

"Not at all," he says while he looks at Derek with concern.

Derek, now rather embarrassed, excuses himself and leaves the table and returns to the bar.

"What was that about?" Mary Ann, leaning past Zac, asks Allison.

"Mommy issues. I'll tell you about it later."

Zac listens and remains calm, trying to reduce the gravity of Derek's seduction disaster.

"Don't worry about it," Adan tells Allison.

"I'm not, now that he has left," she replies.

"He would have had a problem with your shoes anyway," Adan laughs.

"Why, what's wrong with my shoes?" she asks, a little concerned.

"You don't have hang toe." Adan and Zac start laughing at the ladies' confused looks.

"What does that mean?" Mary Ann asks.

"We were having a discussion about women's shoes a while ago," Zac says. "We were wondering why women wear those mile-high open-toe shoes where their toes hang over the front—you know, hang toe."

Zac and Adan laugh again as Allison and Mary Ann cross their arms and sit back in their chairs.

"We want to know if women actually think this is cool or attractive—we don't get it. It looks crappy, and you could damage your toes, or at least your polish. Why do women wear them? Shouldn't you get larger shoes?"

"Well I don't have any," Allison states, knowing she has had them in the past. She stares down at her toes...no hang toe.

Mary Ann wonders if men really notice this sort of thing. "I don't either and never have," she says with confidence, holding up a dancer's leg and showing off one closed-toe black pump. She catches Zac eyeing her leg. He might not be as good-looking as Derek, but no one is. He's tall, with dark windblown hair and a two-day beard, reminding her of her father when she was a kid. It's a rugged look that is very suitable.

"What does Derek do anyway? Who talks like that?" Allison asks.

"He is a trust kid. His dad invented sporks and sold the patent," Adan says. "You know those spoon-fork combinations you get at KFC? Now he just lives in his mom's guesthouse at the family estate."

"It's a huge guesthouse, seven thousand feet," Zac says.

"Go figure," Allison responds.

"What about you?" Mary Ann asks Zac.

"I am an assistant editor for a publishing company," he says with a confident tip of his head.

"And I own an accounting firm," Adan notes, bragging.

"Really, how big is it?" Allison asks, intrigued.

"It's just me," he quips.

"Oh, that's OK." She pats his hand.

"What about you, Mary Ann?" Zac asks with genuine interest.

"I am an elementary-school teacher. I teach third grade," she says, lifting her chin.

"Sounds fun," Zac says.

Before anyone can ask, Allison says, "I'm a fashion designer."

"Really?" Adan asks, excited.

"Yeah, I design shoes for companies like Prada and Gucci," she states, avoiding the truth, knowing she really designs hats for the Kentucky Derby.

Zac and Adan freeze and reach for their martinis in order to avoid more conversation about hang toe.

After the uncomfortable silence, while Mary Ann bites her lip to avoid laughing, she asks if they dance.

"We have and do, but this is a different kind of dancing. What is this?" Adan asks, waving a hand at the couples.

"It is a kind of swing dancing. It is a lot of fun. Would you like to try?" Mary Ann looks directly at Zac.

"Not now. It looks a little complicated," he replies, taking another quick sip of his martini.

"Perhaps you should take some lessons," Allison suggests. "Mary Ann is really good."

Now the guys are uncomfortable, knowing they could get trapped into dancing if they are not careful—and trying to swing dance at the Blue Soul could erase any interest the two women have left in them after Derek's seduction fiasco.

"Maybe we can go dancing after I take some lessons?" Zac asks Mary Ann, trying to avoid being called on the floor tonight but showing definite interest in her.

"OK. There is a dance studio about a mile east from here. It's called Genesis. They teach swing, salsa, and classical styles," she says, hoping Zac is serious.

"OK, we'll check it out," Adan interjects.

"The music here is pretty good, and Saturdays they have swing nights," Allison says. "We both love to swing, so—"

"Cool, swing nights. Did you hear that, Zac?" Adan asks.

"Not that kind of swing, idiot," Zac says, laughing.

Adan decides his earlier tactics with Derek have worked, and he tries flirting a little to see if he can gain Allison's full attention.

She is not interested but remains polite, noticing that Zac and Mary Ann are hitting it off and enclosing each other in the night.

Zac notes that Adan chases one drink after another and becomes completely intoxicated, and he decides Adan has had too much to drink. Not wanting a departure from Mary Ann, he calls a taxi for Adan and sends him on his way.

Allison begins noticing the third-wheel feeling just as she is saved by two more of their friends, Brenda and Ashley.

After the proper introductions, Zac and Mary Ann continue their enchantment, brushing each other's hands accidentally and not so accidentally. Now sitting at a table with four women, Zac does not want to ignore the other three, but at the same time, he wants to fully engage Mary Ann.

"Hey, Hefner, which of these women are yours?" asks a bearded guy with his friend in tow.

"All of them are," Zac replies quickly.

"Yeah, right. I suppose you won't mind if I dance with one of them, would you?"

"I guess not. It's their choice," Zac responds, disappointed and concerned one of the guys will approach Mary Ann.

"Good." The bearded guy turns toward Mary Ann. "Would you like to dance?"

She looks to Zac for approval, knowing she doesn't need it.

"Fine, if you want," he says sharply. As she is escorted to the floor, he thinks he really needs to learn how to swing dance if he is to have any chance with her.

After rounds of the women at his table dancing the night away with other men, Zac finally has an opportunity for some alone time with Mary Ann. While the others dance, he asks, "You want to get out of here?"

"And do what?" she asks with a smile.

"I don't know, but I would like to get to know you better," he says nervously.

"I feel the same." She smiles. "But not tonight." She asks a waitress for a pen and writes her phone number on a napkin and hands it to him. "Let's see if you call me or text me."

CHAPTER 2

Mean

The weekend passes for Zac and Adan. Derek has managed to disappear due to his suave moves that left him alone Friday night. Monday after work, Zac investigates the dance school Genesis. Looking online, he sees it offers swing-dance lessons on Tuesdays and Thursdays. He dials Adan to see if he's still interested in lessons.

"What's up?" Adan asks.

"Dude, I'm calling to see if you want to hit up dance lessons on Tuesday with me," Zac says.

"Yeah. Sure. Why not? I am sure it will be better than impressing women with my alcohol tolerance, or lack of it."

"Good. I signed us up already. I am going to ask Derek too."

"Whatever, dude. I need to go and work on my ledger," Adan says, referring to his women ledger.

"You still have that?" Zac asks.

"Hell yes, since high school," Adan replies.

"Really, dude. Whatever. Later." Zac hangs up and calls Derek.

Derek answers with, "Adan told me I should be more suggestive," as an apology to Zac, who thinks Derek should be apologizing to Allison.

"Yeah, that worked out, didn't it? Hey, I am calling because Adan and I are taking swing-dance lessons Tuesday night. You in?"

"I must decline. I was classically trained since I was five. I think I can hold my own," Derek says with confidence.

"Wow, why don't you ever dance with the hotties then?" Zac responds, shocked.

"The music we have been attacked by at the bars doesn't really accept dancing. Just jump around, and it seems to qualify."

"Yeah, you're right. Well, we are going Tuesday if you want in," Zac reoffers.

"Thanks, but I will not be in attendance."

"OK, see you later."

Tuesday arrives, and Zac begins to wonder if Mary Ann will be there tonight. He pulls her phone number out of his pocket and thinks about calling her. After some thought, he shoves her number back in his pocket. He has not called her yet, and although he wants to, he decides to at least get a lesson in so he can have this be part of the conversation.

Arriving at Genesis, Zac and Adan meet Gino, the short, wiry owner/instructor. Zac looks around, seeing many students but not Mary Ann.

Adan spies the crowd and notices a three-to-one woman-to-man ratio.

"Dude, this couldn't be better," he says.

"Right. Why didn't we think of this?" Zac replies.

Gino pairs Zac and Adan with a couple of women, and the teaching begins. Going through the basics, Zac and Adan both realize this is going to be harder than it looks. They admire some of the better dancers and realize how bad they really might be.

"Zac, if they are here for lessons, we really just suck," Adan says quietly, with a pointing nose.

"Yeah, but it will be OK. We will be fine. Just focus on this and less on the target-rich environment, OK?" They continue the lesson for an hour until it ends.

"What did you guys think?" Gino asks, walking toward them and patting his sweaty neck with a towel.

"Good, I like it," Zac answers, cutting off any comments from Adan.

"This will be my new cardio—" Adan stops midsentence when Zac elbows him.

They head to the Blue Soul for a drink.

Taking a seat at the bar, Zac says, "That was rough."

"Yeah, but so many women. It's perfect," Adan replies as he sits back in a bar chair.

"What can I get you guys?" Thomas asks.

"Couple martinis," Zac informs him.

Thomas starts the martini process as they look around, finding the bar is relatively empty. Two women and three men are the only other patrons.

"You guys look a little drawn," Thomas states while pouring the drinks.

"We took some dance lessons," Adan says eagerly, as if he is some new form of cool.

"Really?" Thomas replies, pouring the last of the martinis.

"Kind of rough—it was more than I expected," Zac concedes.

"Ha. You guys are chasing Allison and Mary Ann," Thomas antagonizes.

"Well maybe, but still, dancing will be good to know for the future." Zac plays it steady.

"Fair enough," Thomas states while looking around at a slow night.

They sit sipping the martinis, listening and relaxing. Nothing is happening—it is a relatively dead night.

Thomas returns and starts washing glasses at the bar sink.

"What's up with the music in here?" Zac asks.

"What do you mean?" Thomas replies.

"This music is from when, the seventies or eighties maybe," Zac notes.

"Yeah, it's better than today's music. Just ask anyone, even the younger crowd," Thomas says as he continues cleaning the glasses.

"Why do you play it?" Adan asks.

"Really? Because class remains and fads fade. I grew up with this. I found that listening to today's current music just bored me. It lacks meaning, caters to some predesigned corporate determination of what is good. The whole music industry has flipped."

"What do you mean? How so?" Zac questions.

"Back in the sixties, seventies, and the beginning of the eighties, what you had was musicians creating bands among themselves. Generally they would get together and create something, and then the record companies would compete to sign these bands so they could record. The Who, the Rolling Stones, Led Zeppelin, the Eagles, Journey, Boston, the Babys, Foreigner, and Blondie were all good or great bands creating music not heard before, differing styles that were good in their own right. Hell, the Commodores, Michael Jackson, even the Bee Gees are all a lot better than today's music. They went out and made it, and then the record companies gave them a shot. I was lucky enough to experience it.

"Now what do we have? Well, in the mid-eighties, record corporations decided to select musicians, put them together for a 'sound' that was proving profitable. Unfortunately for the companies, the sound that had sold started with real creative genius from the artists, not the corporate executives. So sure, we can listen to the same rhythm created in the nineties that persists today with changed lyrics, or we can hear something meaningful. I prefer the latter. Today's music just doesn't have soul. Don't get me wrong—there are some good artists out there that have managed to push through the corporations and make some music. They are far and few between, and fewer stand up to real music from the sixties through the eighties."

"You really think so?" Adan asks.

"Well, just listen. And why are you here? Let me guess. You got tired of some thumping music that was the same bass line? You got burned out on the clubbing scene that offers ringing ears and headaches? You came in here Friday night, met some women, in dresses mind you, and you wonder why I play this music? The best answer is because I like it, and it's my bar."

"Well, it is your bar," Adan comments. Caught in thought about Thomas's opinion of music, they finish their martinis and leave.

The following day Zac and Adan have lunch together.

"I am fucking sore," Zac tells Adan.

"From what? Did you hit the gym yesterday?" Adan laughs, knowing it is from the lessons, because he is sore too.

"No, dude. Those lessons made me move differently."

"Yeah, I know. I'm sore too."

They continue to work on their chicken Caesar salads, regretfully eating healthy, when Adan asks the question Zac has been expecting.

"Did you call Mary Ann?"

"No, not yet."

"What are you waiting for?"

"I was hoping I was going to see her last night." He places his fork down with disappointment.

"Well, you didn't. So call her." Adan sets his fork down and stares at Zac.

"You're right. I am going to call her."

"When?" Adan demands just before taking a drink of his iced tea.

"Now." Zac retrieves her phone number from his pocket.

"You've been carrying her number around like a little girl?" Adan teases.

Zac remains quiet as he dials Mary Ann's number. After quite a few rings, he hears voice mail.

"Hi, Mary Ann. This is Zac. We met last Friday. Call me when you get a chance, OK?"

"Dude, text her. Who calls anymore?" Adan pushes.

"No. That's part of the problem today. No personal contact. Instead, it's full of texts. I would rather have the pleasure of nervous anxiety and wait with anticipation."

"Whatever. What if she doesn't call?" Adan persists.

"I guess we will find out, won't we?" Nervous, Zac reaches for his fork. His phone rings, startling him. He looks and sees it is Mary Ann.

"Well, now we know. Hi, Mary Ann."

"Hi there," she replies, a smile in her voice. "I saw you called and left a message. I could have answered, but I wanted to see if you would leave a message or send me a stupid text."

She now has Zac's attention, after this recent discussion with Adan. "How are you?" he asks.

"Good. I am out for lunch for a couple more minutes before I get back to the kids. How are you?"

"Sore," he says, baiting her interest.

"Sore? From what?"

"Adan and I took swing lessons last night. Fun, and a little more than I expected."

"So you had fun. Did you like it?"

"Yeah, we are going back tomorrow night," Zac says, hoping for a certain response.

"I have to get back. The kids are coming in from lunch recess. Maybe I will see you soon. Thanks for the call. Bye."

Shit, Zac thinks. He didn't have time to ask her out.

"So?" Adan asks with a grin.

"So what?"

"Really, Zac, what are you going to do?"

"Nothing. Maybe I will call her this weekend." Trying not to feel dejected, Zac stands, ready to get back to work.

"OK, I will see you tomorrow night." Adan grins.

Thursday night at Genesis, Adan and Zac return for the second round of lessons. It is a busier night with more students, which suits Adan. He firmly believes this environment, combined with the ratios, can only create additions to his ledger.

Zac scans the room, not finding his choice of partners. Gino enters and begins to partner up similarly experienced students.

Twenty minutes into the lesson, Zac's wish arrives. Mary Ann enters with Allison, and they sit on a bench along the entrance wall. Suddenly nervous, Zac stumbles, and sweat pours profusely down his neck.

Adan notices the two on the bench and smiles, wondering how Zac will handle Mary Ann.

Mary Ann and Allison watch the dancing students with fixed gazes, intentionally pressuring Zac and Adan.

During the next break Zac charges his confidence and approaches Mary Ann and Allison.

"Hi, are you two going to join us or just sit there admiring us?" he asks, smiling and teasing.

"Yes," Mary Ann replies.

"Great, maybe you can show me some stuff out here," Zac says, assuming her acceptance.

"I meant, we will just sit here admiring you."

Mary Ann's laugh pushes Zac into further discomfort.

"You showed up just to watch?" he asks as Adan approaches.

"We weren't sure, so we just stopped in," Allison states to both guys.

"Well, now that you are here, I do believe I owe you the pleasure of my newly found skills," Adan proudly announces to Allison.

"Not tonight, sir."

Zac chooses a more formal request, expecting the proper response. "Mary Ann, would you care to join me on the floor?"

"I don't think so. We've been watching, and I am afraid you might hurt me." She laughs at this disclosure.

Zac refuses to let her escape like she did on the phone. "Would you like to have a drink?" he asks.

"I would."

"Great. We will be done in a while. Would you like to meet in, say, an hour?"

"I did accept, but I can't tonight. I have work tomorrow and some grading to do. How about tomorrow? I am free tomorrow night."

"OK, great. It's a date?" he says, unsure if this should be called a date.

"It is indeed. Tomorrow, seven o'clock at the Blue Soul. We might even dance," she says, smiling.

CHAPTER 3

Learn

*F*riday is here, and Zac is full of anticipation. After work, he gets home to his second-floor one-bedroom apartment overlooking a downtown street and catty-corner to the city's historic one-block park. Entering his apartment directly into the living room, with the kitchen to the right, bathroom to the left, and the bedroom behind the bathroom, he immediately starts stripping his work attire. Throwing his clothes on the bed, he looks at them. Deciding he might actually get lucky tonight, he hangs up his thrown clothes. After a shower, he selects his attire for the night. He is likely to get roped into dancing, so he selects looser-than-normal black dress pants, a maroon dress shirt, a brown leather belt, and oxblood-colored Italian lace-up shoes.

On the way to the Blue Soul, his phone rings. Thinking it might be Mary Ann bailing, he checks and sees it's Adan.

"Hey, what's up?" he answers.

"Derek and I are on our way," Adan says in an antagonizing tone.

"What? You know I have a date with Mary Ann. We don't need an audience," he responds sternly.

"Yeah, I know. Derek called and wanted to check out the Blue Soul again, and I thought it wouldn't hurt to have a wingman."

"I don't need a wingman," Zac replies, still concerned.

"I know, but Derek does."

"Bullshit. You guys just want to see what happens. You know what? It doesn't matter. I will see you guys in a while."

At the Blue Soul, Zac arrives to find Derek and Adan are already sitting at the bar. Walking in, he sees Derek sporting a lavender short-sleeve polo shirt, buttoned up, with a bow tie, gray-and-black plaid golf knickers, no socks, and black wing-tip shoes.

As he approaches the two, he teases, "Styling it tonight, huh, Derek?"

Adan laughs as Derek supports his misunderstood sense of style.

"Yeah, I think I will show the two of you a thing or two about dancing," Derek replies with confidence.

"Can't wait," Adan quips, still laughing at Derek's dress code.

"Have you seen Mary Ann yet?" Zac asks, standing impatiently.

"Not yet," Adan replies, sipping on his martini.

"What time is she to meet you?" Derek formally inquires.

"She said seven."

"Well, it is ten till, so have a drink," Adan says.

Zac orders a martini, wondering what Derek is drinking but is in no way going to ask.

Promptly at seven, Mary Ann enters. Zac sees her out of the corner of his eye but turns away, not wanting to appear eager. She approaches the three and places her hand on Zac's shoulder.

"Hi," she says, smiling.

"Hi, how was your day?" he asks, ignoring Derek and Adan.

Mary Ann wonders if he is really interested or if he's been trained to ask. "Good. You know, snotty third graders."

"Would you care for a drink?" he offers and pats the bar seat beside him.

"Certainly, I'll have a martini also," she says as she notices his. "Can we get a table? I don't hang at the bar unless it's been a bad day that I am going to follow with a bad night."

"Of course. I will follow you." He reaches for the martini Thomas just prepared for her.

Once at the table, Mary Ann asks, "Should we leave those two over there?"

"I am hoping to, but I am sure at some point they will crash our table." Zac places the cocktails on the table and reaches for Mary Ann's chair. He pulls it out, offering her assistance.

"Thank you," she says, appreciating this gesture as she wonders why chivalry died. She flirts with him a bit, touching his arm, letting her fingers slide slowly down his shirt sleeve.

When "Stray Cat Strut" blares out of the speakers, she winks. "Let's see what you have learned."

Anxiety fills him as he has no choice but to accept. They walk to the floor holding hands and start a West Coast swing dance.

Zac has rhythm—he just does not quite know what he is doing. They continue awkwardly because of Zac's limited experience and inability to lead properly. The song ends, and he leads her back to the table, glad he can lead at something.

"Not too bad," she tells him. "We will work on it."

Hearing this excites him. Now he thinks he has a chance to see her more frequently.

As predicted, Derek and Adan do indeed crash the table.

"Not bad. Now I will show you how it's done," Derek states with his unabashed confidence. "Would you care to dance?" he asks Mary Ann.

Zac looks at him with piercing eyes.

"No, thank you." She answers.

Derek is a little stunned.

Mary Ann leans into Zac. "Dressed like that, and after the Allison incident, I am a little afraid of him," she whispers with humor.

"He's harmless and has very limited social skills," he replies. She reaches for his hand with affection and kisses him on the cheek.

Mary Ann and Zac dance to a few more songs and continue with cocktails. Adan and Derek are searching the room for affection of their own when Allison walks in. She sees them and approaches the table.

"I thought you had a date," Mary Ann says.

"Well, not a date like a real date." Allison smiles, flushed and guilty.

Mary Ann does not respond. She knew Allison was meeting a man, but now she knows it was just for the orgasm created with a man, not her hand.

"Good evening." Derek smiles at Allison.

Not one to be rude, she politely replies, "Hi, Derek. Hi, Adan," and she leaves it at that.

Adan is not comfortable with her lack of interest in him, so he slides his chair closer to her. "Can I get you a drink?" Adan asks her.

"Sure, I will have what you are having. Change that. I need a shot. A shot of Jameson." She turns away from the table, looking toward the dance floor.

Adan waves a waitress over and places the necessary order. "Anyone else need anything?" he asks. Derek remains silently confused.

"We're good," Zac states.

Adan orders two shots, thinking this will assist his divide-and-conquer tactic.

The two shots arrive, and Allison thanks Adan. She proceeds to slam the first, then the second. "Thanks, I needed that," she tells Adan, as he looks stumped.

He was sure the second shot was for him. He thinks maybe getting her drunk is the key. "Allison, would you care to dance?" Adan asks.

"No, I wouldn't. I am going to be clear here. I just got laid, and I am not looking for seconds. Furthermore, Adan, I am sure you are a nice guy, but you are too short for me."

Derek smiles, thinking his height is an advantage. Derek builds his confidence and asks Allison to dance.

She looks at him with confusion and anger, then tempers her response. "Not even if I was drunk." She says nothing else.

Adan and Derek now think she is just a bitch, so they turn their attention to other women.

Zac slides closer to Mary Ann as they continue holding hands. Their chemistry is transparent and is now being noticed by the table. Mary Ann takes her hand from Zac's, places it on his thigh, looks at him, and kisses him with full passion. Zac puts his arm around her and pulls her closer.

Allison throws a hotel key card to them. "You can use the room I just used," she laughs.

They collect themselves, flushed without embarrassment.

Derek spies a woman sitting alone at the bar. He excuses himself from the table and approaches her.

She is taken aback by his attire and even more by his stunning looks.

"Hi," he opens nervously.

She looks at him. "What's up?" she asks.

"I noticed you and thought perhaps you would care to dance?" He notices Thomas watching as she contemplates.

"OK." She steps off the bar chair. He escorts her to the floor as the music plays and offers his hand. She takes it, and they begin.

"Wait, check this out," Adan tells the table.

Derek's training begins to show.

"What is he doing?" Mary Ann asks anyone listening. Derek slides and glides his feet without lifting them, like nothing anyone has seen before.

"Oh shit," Zac says, startled.

They continue to watch as Derek reveals his total lack of rhythm and a dance style that insults dancing. The woman is totally shocked and completely uncomfortable. Halfway through the song, she abruptly stops and walks off. She turns to him and thanks him, completely embarrassed, and she races back to the bar.

Derek takes his seat at the table amid smirking and giggling. "I told you I was good," he announces, his confidence unshaken. Shocked silence surrounds the table.

The night is closing, and Adan has given up adding to his ledger. Derek loses interest in the night as well, and they both exit. Allison asks Mary Ann if she needs a ride home, and she declines, explaining she brought her truck.

Zac asks, "Would you like to get out of here?"

"I would. I think I have had it for tonight," she replies.

Zac is not disappointed in her answer. "When can I see you again?" he asks.

"How about Tuesday at Genesis?"

"Sounds great." They walk out together arm in arm. At her Toyota Tacoma, they make out like high-school kids for a few minutes.

"I really should leave," Zac says regretfully, knowing it is the right thing to do.

"I'll see you Tuesday," she confirms.

The weekend passes with each other on their minds. Mary Ann has become interested as has Zac. Tuesday rolls in with both anticipating seeing each other.

Zac and Adan arrive ten minutes early at Genesis. Mary Ann stands in form-fitting yoga pants, talking to Gino. She notices their arrival and excuses herself. She passes Adan with a "hi," then reaches out for Zac. They embrace in a huge hug, and she kisses him on the neck.

"I had fun Friday night," she says, snuggling under the arm around her shoulder.

"I did too. It's great to see you. Now let's see if I can get better tonight."

Gino announces the lesson will begin with a Lindy Hop, a quick dance from the '20s and '30s jazz era.

After half an hour of dancing, correcting, correcting, and more correcting, Zac decides he is going to dip her at the end of the next song. As the song reaches its end, he presses into her. Recognizing what is about to happen, she reluctantly gives in. He starts the dip as his right arm lowers to her waist. She reclines, curving her back. His arm falls too low and finds its place on her butt. She feels what is happening and tenses. She falls back onto her head, her outside leg sweeping past his head, her inside leg following as her knee collapses his arm and collides with Zac's chin, knocking him out as she falls to the side.

Rolling from the collapse to the floor, her neck twists. She looks over to Zac. He starts bleeding from his chin and is out cold. Gino races to the disaster. The crowd surrounds them, and Adan tries to wake Zac.

"Are you OK?" Adan asks Mary Ann.

She complains of pain in her neck as Zac wakes from this mishap.

"Dude, what happened?" he asks, looking at Adan.

"I don't know. I didn't see it."

"You dropped me on my head," Mary Ann moans.

"Oh shit, are you OK?" Zac sits up, checking on her.

"I don't know. My neck really hurts."

Zac is dripping blood from the one-inch gash in his chin, and Gino offers a towel.

Concerned, Adan says, "Dude, you need stiches. Mary Ann, you need to be checked out. I am taking you two to the hospital." Both are too shaky to refuse.

Zac's red badge of courage is ten stiches on the lower right of his chin. Mary Ann now has the comfort of a spongy neck brace. As they leave the hospital, Mary Ann reaches for Zac's hand, and they hold hands.

"I could use a drink," Mary Ann announces.

"Me too," Zac replies, trying to figure out how this went so wrong. "Do you want to go to the Blue Soul?"

"No, I would like to relax a little. How about we go back to your place? Do you have any liquor?"

"Yeah, I can make us a drink," he states without any real sexual tension between them, due to the disaster of the evening.

They enter his apartment, and she takes a seat on the couch in the living room. She sits as comfortably as she can with her neck brace and is facing the kitchen.

"I have some Chopin vodka. Straight, or would you prefer a martini?" he asks.

"On ice is fine."

He places some ice cubes in a couple of glasses and fills them. He hands her the drink and sits next to her. "What happened?" he asks.

"You dropped me on my head. When you did, my knee hit your chin and took you out."

"Shit, I am sorry. I guess I need more work. I hope you are OK." He hopes she accepts his clumsiness.

"I think I will be OK. I'll have a bruise on my knee. You were knocked out cold. I hope you don't have a concussion. The stiches are cute though." She lightens up now, relaxing.

"Yeah. This explanation won't be much fun," he teases.

"Oh, is it going to suck telling your friends your girlfriend knocked you out and gave you stiches?" she teases back. Then she realizes the mistake in her words.

"Girlfriend?" he drawls.

They both remain silent for a minute, looking into and stirring their full drinks, unsure how to respond. At the same time, they both slam the vodka to its end. Looking at each other, they smile and laugh. Almost a race, they both finish at the same moment. Mary Ann smiles again yet refuses to say anything, and she stares at Zac. His smile begins to stretch his stiches. Simultaneously, they grab each other and begin making out, with pain in Mary Ann's neck and Zac's chin.

Kissing and feeling each other, they begin to peel each other's clothes off. Dropping shoes and shirts to the floor, they rise and make their way to the bedroom. Naked by the time they get to the bed, Mary Ann lies on her back, accepting. The pillow crunches and creates pain in her neck. She reaches behind her with one arm and throws it across the room. Zac climbs on top of her with obvious passion and blood flow. Their combined lust and passion are interrupted by Mary Ann's head hitting the headboard, sending a jolt of pain though her neck.

He slides her down the bed. They slow down and continue having sex with passion, not just fucking. Mary Ann's eyes close, her body writhing. Zac notices a small blood smear on her cheek. Fuck it, he thinks as they continue. The combination of hot and passionate sex sends them over the edge to completion. Zac looks down at Mary Ann, admiring her. He notices half her face is now smeared in blood.

"Oh shit, you have blood on your face."

"Yeah, I think you tore a stitch."

He climbs out of bed to retrieve a towel and cleans her face, then his. He lies with her, her head on his shoulder, albeit with the awkwardness of the neck brace. "Yeah, my girlfriend did this," he says.

She looks up at him, smiling. "Well, if you are my boyfriend, you will have to take care of me tonight."

"Of course, I insist you stay the night with me so I can watch over you," he teases.

CHAPTER 4

Three

*A*fter a couple of months, Mary Ann and Zac begin to isolate themselves in their relationship. Zac's dancing improves, yet Mary Ann seems to have developed some fear or lack of trust with this. Their chemistry is undeniable, as all their friends have concluded they belong together. Both begin to realize the inevitability of the relationship, as her dresser drawer has become half of his closet. The majority of their time together is spent at Zac's apartment. His location is closer to downtown and the elementary school.

As they lie together in bed on a Sunday morning, the elephant in the room becomes the discussion. "Honey, what are we going to do?" Mary Ann asks.

"About what?" he asks in return, knowing full well what her question is.

"We always stay at your place, and mine is collecting cobwebs," she states cutely.

"I know. I love you…staying here," he carefully states. He understands this is a crucial point in their relationship and is careful to proceed.

"I love…staying here," she says with a smile.

They both realize what is about to be said. They are just unwilling to be the first, even if it is mutual. Zac does not want her to feel like she is pushing herself in but is a little unsure if this is too early to live together. He hugs her, full of affection. "What would you like to do?" he asks as he kisses her on the forehead.

"If we lived together, we would save rent money. We both work closer to your place than mine, and we like to hang out downtown. There's more to do, and you are blocks from the Blue Soul and numerous restaurants," she points out.

"I agree." Zac pulls her closer.

They both think they are trying to talk each other and themselves into this with sound reasoning. They have known each other for about three months and are concerned with the speed this relationship is taking. After a few wordless moments, Zac makes a decision. "When would you like to move in? It would be easier to be here. Hell, half your stuff is here, and you already make me put the toilet seat down," he teases, trying to make this easy.

"Like that is such a problem." She giggles. "Is next weekend OK?" she asks nervously, not wanting to be pushy.

"Yes." They embrace in meaningful, sensual Sunday-morning sex.

The week passes with Mary Ann staying with Zac every night. They have accepted their decision and are now excited about it. Neither has told their friends yet. They have decided to tell Allison, Derek, and Adan together Friday night at the Blue Soul.

Zac and Mary Ann strut into the Blue Soul Friday night ahead of their friends. They select the table furthest from the dance floor, and both begin with a martini. Adan and Derek arrive together. They find Mary Ann and Zac, yet meander to them so they can view the possible targets for the night. As they sit, the waitress takes their order.

"I will have a rum runner," Derek almost yells.

"I am going to start slow. I will have a Dos Equis," Adan says.

Just then, Allison walks in and catches the waitress to order a martini.

"We have some news," Mary Ann informs the table.

"You're pregnant," Derek blurts.

"No, I am not," she replies, holding up her martini.

Allison digs into Derek with her eyes, as Adan shakes his head.

"Mary Ann is moving in with me," Zac states, staring at Derek.

"Nice. You two are great together. Congratulations." Adan shakes hands with Zac.

"You two are not even married," Derek says.

"Shut the fuck up," Allison tells him with her hand raised like she is about to backhand him.

Stunned, Derek slides his chair further from Allison and closer to Adan.

"Maybe you should shut the fuck up," Adan says while he winks at Allison.

She rolls her eyes at him, laughing. Allison leans to Mary Ann. "Are you sure about this?" she asks.

Leaning back, Mary Ann replies, "Yes. We are really great together, and I am at his place all the time anyway."

"OK then, when do we redecorate your new place?" Allison asks, excited.

Mary Ann laughs and returns her attention to Zac.

"Waitress, we need shots all the way around," Adan orders.

"No, we don't," Zac counters. "We are making this an early night because we are moving her in tomorrow." They finish their martinis and leave for "home," while Derek and Adan peruse the scene for the night and try to figure out how to ditch Allison.

Once Mary Ann's personal items are situated in the apartment, she and Zac sit on the couch, watching a movie. Mary Ann reaches for her beer and looks to the corner to the right of the window and left of the television. This vacant area by the window in front of the counter top separating the kitchen from the living room is the perfect spot for a chair.

"Honey, I want to get a chair for the window. Then I can read there and grade papers with the natural light."

Completely unaware of any real redecorating notions, Zac agrees mindlessly.

"Can you get out of work early tomorrow? And can we take a look at some? I am off at noon for a teachers' in-house meeting, but I feel a cold coming on." She laughs and fakes a cough.

"OK, sure. I'll dive early, and we will get you a chair." He smiles, wanting her happiness.

"Let's have lunch and make an afternoon out of it," she suggests.

"OK, whatever you want, baby," he says as he hugs her.

After Thursday's lunch, they begin their quest. Shopping at numerous stores, they stop at Internal Design, and she finally sees her chair, a classic nail-front armchair finished in an indigo fabric. She sits in it, running her hands along the arms and feeling the fit, testing the comfort.

"Try it," she begs Zac.

"Do you like it?" he asks, smiling down at her.

"I love it."

"Then I don't need to try it. We'll take it," he says to the hovering salesman.

"I will check stock and be right back." The salesman positions himself at the infamous computer behind the counter. He weaves his way to Mary Ann's armchair and mentions the inevitable good and bad news. "The bad news is I don't have one here in storage. The good news is I can have one from our warehouse tomorrow."

Zac thinks this is always the case and wonders why a buyer can't just take a piece of furniture home. The salesman probably wants a commission too, so what is this about?

Seeing the look on Zac's face, Mary Ann cuts him off. "Can we pick it up Saturday? We're both working tomorrow," she asks, standing and then perching herself on the chair's arm.

"Sure. Let's take care of the paper work." The salesman walks toward the mysterious computer that said her chair was not immediately available. Mary Ann reaches into her purse, a Gucci lavender tote, and pulls out her credit card.

"No, I got this," Zac insists, grabbing her butt.

"But…but…"

"No. This is for you, and I insist." He smiles indulgently, hoping he receives a wet kiss right there at the counter.

"Thank you." She kisses the scar on his chin. They collect the invoice and decide a night in is in order.

Friday afternoon the salesman calls Zac and informs him of the completely expected problem. Internal Design didn't have the chair at the warehouse that the mysterious computer showed in the inventory. However, the salesman says they can have the one in the showroom if they choose to take it. Zac agrees and passes on the information to Mary Ann that night.

Saturday is here, and they are off to collect Mary Ann's chair. On the way, in Mary Ann's ten-year-old beat-up Toyota Tacoma she received from her father at college graduation, they stop at the grocery store to pick up a few groceries. Exiting the store, they both pass an exhibit featuring rescue dogs. Seeing this, Zac stops to take a look. Mary Ann thinks these are designed to play the hearts of women yet stays by his side. Four makeshift cages hold four to five dogs each.

Zac says he loves dogs and kneels to examine them. He notices one sitting at the back of one of these cages. All the other dogs are excited, but this one is shaking and obviously scared, sitting alone at the rear. "Look at that little guy," he says. "What's up, little guy?" The other dogs try to capture his attention. The little Border Terrier looks up at him and then puts his head down.

Mary Ann succumbs to this little guy and kneels next to Zac. "What's wrong?" she asks.

"What's the story with that little guy in the back?" Zac asks the woman in charge.

"I don't know. He must have been abused," the woman responds. She opens the cage, picks up the terrier, and hands him to Zac.

Still shaking, the dog nervously licks Zac on the chin. "Oh, you poor little guy." He looks to Mary Ann for approval.

She leans in to see the scared terrier. He looks up at her and kisses her chin also. "OK, you are going home with us," she says as the little dog buries his head in Zac's arms.

"He is a Border Terrier, right?" he asks the woman.

"I think he is a Border Terrier. He looks like one."

"Do you know how old he is?"

"Based on his teeth, he is about four years old."

They complete the necessary paper work for the adoption and go back into the store with the dog to retrieve the necessary food and a leash. Walking out, they pass a kiosk with puppy stickers. Zac looks through them and selects an "I love my Border Terrier" round sticker with a picture of the dog in the middle. They arrive at Mary Ann's truck, and Zac sticks it to the middle of the rear window. Mary Ann says nothing, silently agreeing to his actions.

Arriving at the furniture store with the little guy sitting in Zac's lap, he hands their new pet to Mary Ann and enters Internal Design. He returns with directions to pick up the chair at the rear of the store.

Back at the apartment Zac manages to get the chair up the stairs and in the apartment alone, while Mary Ann unloads the groceries. Zac positions the armchair, angling it in the corner with the daylight drowning it.

Zac sits on the couch with Mary Ann. The little terrier sniffs the chair and jumps onto it, looking at them for approval.

"What should we name him?" Mary Ann asks.

Like a bolt from the sky, Zac blurts, "Jake."

When he hears the name, the little terrier perks his ears, looking at them.

"Well, I guess that's it, Jake," Mary Ann confirms, and his little ears perk up again. Jake, obviously still scared and unsure of his new surroundings, just lies on the chair, gazing at them.

After dinner, the two snuggle on the couch, admiring their acquisitions. Jake notices them looking his direction and whines ever so lightly.

"Oh, you poor little guy," Mary Ann says, just above a whisper. "Jake, come here." Jake looks up, clearly both excited and confused. "Come here," she calls again. Jake slowly stands up. "Come on," she encourages as Zac watches.

Jake jumps off the chair and walks to them slowly, with his ears up and tail down. She reaches down and lifts him to her lap. Mary Ann and Jake kiss each other. She turns to watch the television, Jake sitting in her lap.

Zac reaches for Mary Ann's left hand. He notices that Jake starts to calm, feeling their love. Jake spies Mary Ann's right hand and begins pawing at it repeatedly. She puts her open hand out, and Jake places his paw in it and looks toward the television. Now he is holding her hand also.

"Look at this little guy," she tells Zac.

"I know—cute, huh?" he whispers in her ear.

She moves Jake off her lap and situates him so he's sitting on their thighs between them. She reaches into her purse, pulls out her phone, and takes a selfie of the three of them. Jake lies down and falls asleep.

CHAPTER 5

Conflict

A couple of weeks after the chair and Jake acquisitions, Mary Ann and Allison have lunch at their regular grill.

"So how's it going?" Allison asks, referring to the new living arrangements.

"Good. Jake has settled in, and Zac bought me a new chair so I can read and grade papers by the window."

"He bought you a chair?" Allison sits up, alarmed. "Why? Couldn't you buy it?"

"Yeah, but he insisted. What's wrong with that?" Mary Ann feels she needs to defend her relationship. She leans back slightly in her chair as the waitress sets her spinach salad in front of her.

"He doesn't own you. Or does he?" asks Allison as she spreads her napkin.

"No. We're together, and I think he thought it would be nice," Mary Ann says, stabbing some spinach with a fork.

"All right, but I will be sure no man takes care of me," Allison responds angrily.

"What's the problem? Why are you mad? Zac bought me a chair, big deal. It was a nice thing to do since I moved into his place. I think he wanted me to feel comfortable. Why is it a problem?" Mary Ann replies with hurt feelings.

"It isn't. Sorry, I guess I am out of line." They finish their quick lunch without many more words and return to their jobs.

Back at home after work, Mary Ann is grading in her chair with Jake lying on the back. His legs sprawled and hanging from each side, he has found his new place.

Zac opens the door and steps in. "Hey, baby, how are you? Jake, are you being a good boy?"

Jake jumps off the chair, bouncing off Mary Ann's lap, and runs to the leash hanging on the wall.

"Hi, honey, how was your day?" Mary Ann asks.

"Good, same shit, you know. I am going to take Jake for a walk. Want to join?" Zac reaches for the leash and bends to attach it to Jake's collar.

"No, baby, I am going to start dinner."

"OK, we will be back soon."

After Zac and Jake leave, Mary Ann sets down the papers she was grading and reflects on her conversation with Allison, wondering about the meaning behind the conversation.

She rises and starts toward the kitchen. Stopping in the kitchen she questions why Zac did not want to know about her day and didn't at least ask. Looking at the dinner task, she thinks to herself, is this what I am becoming?—referring to making dinner and Zac buying her a chair. She calms as she opens the refrigerator and grabs a beer. Feeling some resentment she does not understand, she opens the beer and guzzles it from the bottle.

After dinner the two are sitting on the couch with some music on, and Mary Ann's agitation creeps in. It is unintended, and she doesn't really know why, except that maybe such thoughts were sparked by her conversation with Allison. Now she feels like she's questioning everything, including Allison's instigation.

"Why did you buy me that chair?" she blurts, turning to face Zac.

"I thought you wanted it," he responds, surprised.

"I do, but is there another reason?" She wonders why she can't just let it go.

"No. You wanted it, and I wanted to buy it for you. I can afford it, and..." Reaching for his beer, he is now further alarmed and wonders what's going on. After a few minutes of silence that Zac refuses to break, he feels Mary Ann starting to calm down.

"OK. Thank you. I love it."

Now Zac is thoroughly confused. He notices that Jake, lying on the back of the chair, watches them with one eye open. He is likely confused too, Zac thinks.

The week continues, with this seed planted by Allison starting to grow. Mary Ann continues to try to kill it and let it go, her own internal struggle. She knows this is not about Zac and does not want to push it on him.

After work on Friday, before Zac arrives home, Mary Ann's seed is growing and starting to upset her. She decides to call Allison to straighten this out. She dials her phone.

Allison answers, "Hey, I am still at work. What's going on?"

"I want to know what you meant by our conversation at lunch the other day," says a hurt and mad Mary Ann.

"Nothing. I just didn't think you were the kind of woman who would let a man take care of her," Allison responds.

"I am not being taken care of. I am in a relationship with Zac, and you make it sound like because he is a man, I have a problem." Mary Ann is hurt, confused, and conflicted.

"That's not what I said and not what I mean. I am really busy. Can we talk about this later?"

"Sure." As Mary Ann hangs up, Jake jumps off the chair toward her, looking for some TLC. She kisses Jake's nose as Zac opens the door.

"Hi, baby," she says as she reaches for a kiss. Zac complies eagerly. "Can you take Jake out?" she asks.

"Sure, love to." He grabs the leash and ties it to Jake. "Come on, big guy," he says as Jake jumps in circles.

They leave, and Mary Ann sits in her chair. She thinks about how she just asked Zac to take Jake out. She questions herself about becoming "that kind of woman" and sulks momentarily, until she realizes she loves her new chair. The weekend is here.

Saturday morning, Jake wakes them, obviously full of ambition and not quite sure how to direct it. Mischief is in his mind. Zac and Mary Ann wonder what the bouncing energy is about. He sits between them, looking at them with guilty eyes.

"What are you doing?" Zac asks. Jake jumps between their heads, grabs the blankets, and struggles to pull them to the bottom of the bed. As the cool air brushes Mary Ann's body, she reaches to stop the coup and finds herself in a blanket tug-of-war with ten pounds of Jake, who refuses to give in. Zac starts laughing and decides his help would be appreciated. Instead of joining the tug-of-war, he just reaches out and picks up Jake to end the battle. Mary Ann realizes her foolishness and laughs along, hugging and kissing them both.

Mary Ann decides she should take Jake for a walk and asks Zac to make breakfast. Zac readily agrees and heads for the kitchen while Mary Ann and Jake leave the apartment.

They walk to the historic park catty-corner from the apartment building. As Jake tugs Mary Ann along, she feels like they're having a bonding moment. Jake does his business, and Mary Ann throws the bag in a garbage pail. Jake notices a couple sitting on a park bench and struts in front of them.

"How cute," the woman says to Mary Ann. Jake, as if on cue, rushes her leg and immediately starts humping it with his tongue hanging.

"Jake, stop that," Mary Ann commands, and he sits at her feet.

"Little rodent," the man says, and Jake turns and bites the bottom of his pant leg off and starts running away. Mary Ann apologizes as she is dragged by the same ten pounds.

Entering the apartment, Jake still has the torn pant piece in his mouth, like it is a trophy for the day. "Look what the little shit did to some guy in the park," Mary Ann tells Zac raggedly.

"What's up with you today?" Zac asks Jake as he pours food into Jake's dish. Jake drops the pant piece and digs in.

As he serves breakfast, Zac asks Mary Ann about her plans for the day.

"None, how about you?" she replies.

"Going to hit the gym. I was thinking maybe we could go out tonight. We haven't been out in a while. We do still have friends, you know." Zac thinks going out and having fun will be good for them.

"Sure, how about dinner and then the Blue Soul?" she replies.

"Cool, I will call Adan and Derek and see if they are going out tonight. Call Allison—maybe she will want to go," he says.

"OK." She wonders momentarily about her conflict with Allison. Is it a conflict with Allison or a conflict within?

After dinner, they arrive at the Blue Soul. Adan and Derek are sitting at the bar, a couple of drinks into the night. Allison has not arrived yet.

"Hey, guys," Zac says as they join Derek and Adan.

"Lovebirds, how are you two doing?" Adan asks, smirking.

"We're good. Let's get a table." Zac gestures behind him.

"Sure. Is Allison coming?" Derek asks.

"She said she was," Mary Ann answers.

They make their way to a table centered in front of the dance floor and take their seats.

While dancing with Mary Ann, Zac notices she is a little off. He wonders what is going on, since she is clearly better than him. Not quite willing to follow his lead, it actually leads to rather hapless engagements on the floor. He lets it go, thinking anyone can have an off day.

Adan, as usual, is in pursuit of the many, still not realizing the best way to hunt is to select one target. He apparently thinks all the other women he chases will not notice. Derek is sipping a piña colada through a straw, full of his normal confidence. The night slows, with Adan striking out and Derek awaiting any of the women to approach him. Zac and Mary Ann call it a night.

Back at the apartment, Jake is atop his claimed spot. Mary Ann and Zac climb into bed and engage in passionate sex. They're oblivious to Jake leaping onto the bed, and they continue in the missionary position, moaning passionately. Jake, feeling ignored, makes his move. He crawls slowly up the bed to the right of Zac, crawling like a sniper avoiding detection every inch along the way. He reaches their heads and decides he wants in. He leans into their kissing and engages them both with his own kisses.

"What are you doing?" Zac asks, frustrated.

"Go on," Mary Ann tells Jake. He backs off, turns, and takes a couple of steps toward the middle of the bed and parks his butt.

Zac and Mary Ann continue, as they never stopped. Jake starts pawing at Mary Ann's hand.

"What are you doing?" she asks, looking down to her left.

"Fucking. You really didn't know?" Zac responds.

"Not you. Jake," she says as she puts out her hand for Jake. He places his paw in it.

"Really, Jake?" Zac asks. Jake ignores him. He is happy now that he has Mary Ann's hand.

"Whatever, honey. Keep going." Mary Ann keeps the rhythm. Upon completion, Zac lies on top of Mary Ann, catching his breath. Jake pulls his paw from Mary Ann and bites Zac lightly on the right butt cheek—not drawing blood, just an attention-getter.

"What the fuck, you little guy. A little attitude today, huh?" Zac asks Jake.

Mary Ann laughs and calls Jake to her side, and Zac rolls off her.

Monday during lunch Mary Ann calls Allison. She is unwilling to let go of her comments from last week's lunch.

"Sorry I couldn't make it the other night," Allison says.

"Is everything OK?" Mary Ann asks.

"Yeah, I was just a little busy. It ended up, and I do mean *up*, longer than I thought, so I stayed longer. Oh hell, I stayed the night," she reveals.

Mary Ann, still miffed by Allison's earlier comments, says, "So I guess you needed a man?"

"No, I didn't need a man. I wanted one," Allison sternly replies, knowing where Mary Ann is directing the conversation.

"Does he take care of you?" Mary Ann asks Allison.

"Not like you're taken care of," Allison snipes back.

"You know," Mary Ann says firmly, "I can be my own woman and want a man too. You insinuate it's one or the other. Seems to me that you are using men for sex. Something you

49

accuse men of all the time and use to solidify your position." Mary Ann is upset with this double standard.

"I am sorry. It wasn't my intention to question you, or even Zac, or your relationship. It just caught me off guard that you have let him take the lead. I am really sorry," Allison says without remorse in her voice.

Mary Ann doesn't know what to do. She recognizes that Allison has pulled her strings and hangs up without saying good-bye.

CHAPTER 6

Trust

*T*he next few weeks find Mary Ann struggling with Allison's comments and internally questioning herself about them. Her confusion lies in being her own woman while being in a relationship with Zac. She wonders if moving in with Zac was the right move or simply convenient. His salary is larger than hers, and his desire to take care of the majority of the financial obligations concerns her. She does not question the chemistry they possess or how much she cares for him. She is caught up in becoming "that woman" and refusing to let it happen.

Zac notices a distance in Mary Ann. He is unsure of her and becomes insecure about their relationship. Deciding not to push her, he gives her space.

Mary Ann has also come to the realization that she needs some space to clear up her internal confusion.

The weekend arrives, and Zac and Mary Ann decide to hit the Blue Soul for some stress relief. Attempting to make the night about them, they do not inform their friends of the night out. While dancing, Mary Ann and Zac aren't on the same page, and it becomes noticeable to both of them. Frustrated, Zac instigates the situation, questioning Mary Ann.

"What's going on?" he asks, dejected.

"I don't know. We just can't seem to get it together," she replies.

"We both know you are better than this. You won't let me lead, so we are scattered," he informs her, concerned.

"Is that what this is about? You leading?" she asks.

Zac is oblivious to her real question. "Isn't that how this works? Isn't the man supposed to lead?"

"I guess so," she says, detached.

Zac starts toward the table and finishes his latest martini. "Let's get out of here. This isn't working tonight," he says.

"Taking the lead, huh?" she responds with anger.

Stunned, Zac stands, but Mary Ann remains seated. His confusion with her is making him defensive. "Are you ready?" he asks.

"Sure," she states, not wanting to escalate the conversation.

At home, Zac thinks maybe this night was not meant to be and decides to go straight to bed. Mary Ann, struggling with the "lead" comments of the night, along with Allison's planted seed, sits in her chair with Jake in her lap. She can feel the tension in the air permeating into Jake. She falls asleep in her chair, Jake still on her lap.

The sunlight breaking through the window wakes both Jake and Mary Ann. Realizing she did not go to bed, she feels a creeping guilt. She wonders why she is treating Zac like this. She feels lousy about it. He knows nothing of her quandary, and he has been nothing but the best to her. She follows Jake when he jumps off her lap and struts straight to the bedroom and jumps on the bed, finding Zac already awake. Mary Ann slowly walks to bed and crawls in next to the two of them.

Silence can be heard in the room. Neither wants to break its painful existence. Jake takes the lead by kissing them both and jumping all over them in his own obvious attempt to liven the situation.

"I am sorry, babe," she states sadly.

"About what? What's going on?" he asks, afraid.

"I don't know," she replies, knowing exactly what the problem is. She doesn't accept that it is her problem, just a problem.

"Let me know when you do. I am going to the gym after I take Jake for a walk." He pops out of bed, pissed off. How can he fix a problem he doesn't know exists? Jake jumps over Mary Ann and off the bed, running to his leash. Zac dresses in some sweats and exits the bedroom to meet Jake.

The weekend concludes with the silence of a wake. At work Monday, Zac's thoughts are tied up by Mary Ann. He struggles with his complete lack of knowing what is going on with her. The typical questions trace his thoughts. Did he do something wrong? If so, what? And why wouldn't she discuss it with him? Should he confront her? Would this help, hurt, or make any difference? He finally kicks his mental ass and decides to call Adan and see if he has time for lunch. Adan agrees, unaware of Zac's frame of mind.

Sitting down for lunch, Adan asks, teasing, "What's up? You and Mary Ann ready for marriage?"

"I don't know. She has been weird lately," Zac informs Adan with displeasure.

"Maybe she is on her period," Adan replies, trying to be humorous.

"Yeah, I think I would know if she was. I don't think so." Zac reaches for his water.

"Something's up, huh?" Adan asks.

"Yeah, but I don't know what. She has been really distant, like something is bugging her."

Adan remains quiet, allowing Zac to vent.

"We went dancing last Friday, and it was a mess. We couldn't get shit right. I asked her about it, and she was full of attitude. It was like she was fighting me on the floor. Then she got pissed because I questioned her about allowing me to lead. I don't know what's up."

"Well, you did drop her on her head," Adan says, laughing.

"Yeah, but that's not it. I think we need some space. Maybe a guys' night out. I could use it, and maybe she needs some girl time. I don't know."

"All right, when do you want to get out? I'll call Derek."

"I'll let you know," Zac says, semi-relieved.

"How is Jake?" Adan asks.

"He's got some attitude lately. Stirring up shit, he seems to be quite the character. He's cool. I love that little guy," Zac relays with a smile.

"OK, give me a call about getting out. I could use some additions to my ledger."

"Really, you're still on that?" Zac asks, thinking about his single days.

"Fuck, yeah. Every woman, phone numbers, dates, what the sex was like—hell, even their toenail colors," Adan says, laughing.

"That's wrong. What are you going to do with it?" Zac asks with interest.

Adan shrugs. "Don't know. Maybe it just makes me feel good. Going to try to fill the book up." He grins at Zac.

"All right, what happens if you find yourself in a relationship, and she asks how many women you have been with? Or worse, what if she finds your ledger? Are you going to tell her the exact number or about how good it makes you feel?"

Adan stays quiet for a few moments. "Shit, I never thought about that. I keep it at work anyway, so whatever."

"What would you do if Allison got her hands on it?" Zac asks, knowing she rejected Adan.

"Fuck her. She is too tall for me anyway."

"Yeah, right, dude. You would tag her if you had the chance, and you know it. The problem is you two are exactly alike, just not the same height," Zac says, laughing.

"Fuck off. I won't give her a taste," Adan replies with his own laughter, feeling uncomfortable.

"All right, dude. I will call you about getting out," Zac says in an attempt to lighten the mood.

Back at the office, Zac decides Wednesday night he and the boys are going out. He calls Adan and gives him the news. Adan is certainly on board.

Wednesday rolls in, and after work, on his way home, Zac picks up a dozen roses for Mary Ann. He thinks this is at least a peace offering and hopes it will soften the blow when he tells her about hanging with the boys. He opens the door and finds Mary Ann dressed for a night out.

"Hi, baby, I thought you might like these," he says as he hands her the roses.

"They are beautiful. Thank you, honey," she replies with her smile. "I am going out tonight for some girl time with Allison. We need to catch up. Are you OK with that?" she asks, frustrated that she did.

Zac is a little shocked but takes advantage. "Yeah. I was going to tell you I am going out with the boys tonight. I am meeting Derek and Adan at Joey's Bar."

"OK. I am late, so I will see you later," she tells Zac as she primps for a second before leaving. She kisses Zac on the cheek as she reaches for the door.

"Bye. I will take Jake out before I get out of here." He realizes she is gone before his sentence is finished. Jake jumps off the chair, straight to his hanging leash. Walking Jake, Zac begins to wonder if he and Mary Ann are on the same page or if there is some alternate motive. Back at the apartment, he feeds Jake and notices the roses lying on the counter top. Disappointed, he selects a vase from the cabinet, cuts the stems, fills the vase with water, and arranges them in it. He then leaves for the bar.

Meanwhile, Allison arrives early at the Blue Soul, unsure of the pending discussions. She orders a shot of Jameson, slams it, then another. She believes this will help with her nerves and calm her before Mary Ann arrives.

Mary Ann walks in and locates Allison at a table in the back corner, far from the dance floor.

"Hi there," Allison greets her.

"Hi. What are we drinking?" Mary Ann asks, taking the seat across from Allison.

"Choose your poison, beautiful," Allison responds with a compliment designed to soften.

"Shots," Mary Ann says as she waves the waitress over and orders the necessary slingers. "How are you?" she asks Allison, trying to control the conversation.

"It's been a rough week," Allison replies in attempt to play on Mary Ann's feelings.

"I'm sorry. Me too. I am not sure what to do about Zac."

"What do you mean? I thought this was perfect."

"I find myself becoming 'that woman.' I love him, but I don't love the idea of being the wifey," she informs Allison.

The shots arrive, and Mary Ann immediately orders two more. They slam the shots and continue the discussion.

"I did not mean to attack your fortitude when it comes to Zac—though that's what I did. I was wrong. I see how you two are together, and maybe I am a little jealous. I am so sorry, and I hope you won't throw this away on account of me," Allison relates solemnly.

"What I have with Zac was really special—"

"Was?" Allison interrupts.

"Yeah, but things are off right now, and I don't know how to reconcile who I am with what I am becoming. It is really weighing on me. I am distant. Every time he is nice to me, I think he is trying to control me or own me. I don't know. I know I am screwed in the head right now."

"Wait, did you say you love him?" Allison asks happily.

They slam the next two shots, and Mary Ann orders two more, trying to numb herself—not realizing Allison had two prior to her arrival.

"Yes, I did, and I do. He is great at being a man, but that doesn't mean he can do everything for me."

"Have you told him?"

"No."

Allison is speechless for once, and her head is beginning to spin after four shots in fifteen minutes.

"What do you think?" Mary Ann asks.

"I don't know. I think Zac is great. His only negatives are Adan and Derek," she responds, laughing.

"Yeah, they are harmless, but sometimes they are fun to watch. You know, how Derek fucks shit up with the ladies, and Adan tries to fuck all the ladies on earth. Poor guys," Mary Ann says, laughing.

"I think I am getting drunk." Allison slouches in her chair.

"Good, I will catch up." Mary Ann giggles as she orders four shots, two each.

Zac, Adan, and Derek show up at Joey's Bar, a little dive that holds no more than forty patrons. Entering the bar, they find it is ladies' night, to the pleasure of Derek and Adan. Zac could care less. As the night progresses, Zac is not interested in discussing his relationship and runs wingman for Adan, as it looks like he has the interest of a woman. Derek has many women approach him—only to run for cover after a short conversation.

Mary Ann arrives home before Zac, completely drunk. Barely able to remove her shoes, she accomplishes the task and falls in bed, which spins and spins and spins. She sits up and places one foot on the ground. It doesn't work as her mouth salivates. She bounces off the walls to the bathroom and holds her hair as she gets the privilege of retracing the shots of the night.

Zac walks in to the delight of this sight. He offers to hold her hair while she seeks the bottom of the toilet.

"Leave me alone." She fights him off. "I can do it."

Shocked, hurt, and even offended, he leaves her to her choices and crawls in bed. Jake witnesses the events sadly and lies next to Mary Ann on the bathroom floor, to protect her as she passes out.

Thursday morning, the epic hangover drives Mary Ann's head into a wall as she wakes on the bathroom floor with Jake by her side. She rubs him gently as Zac makes breakfast for the three of them.

"Babe, breakfast is served," Zac yells in a whisper. Jake runs to his dish to find he gets bacon and eggs this morning!

"Thanks."

Hurt, Zac leaves without good-byes. Mary Ann collects herself and decides a substitute teacher is required for her class.

For Zac, the only pleasure of the weekend is spending more time with Jake as Mary Ann sinks in her chair, grading papers and then reading one book after another. Days pass, and both are unwilling to discuss the elephant in the room. Unfortunately, Zac doesn't know what the problem is, just that there definitely is one. Both are in bed early, every sexless night.

The pressured days crash into another weekend. On Saturday, Mary Ann finds herself cleaning the apartment while Zac is at the gym. She notices the roses have died. She stops in a moment of reflection, wondering if the roses reflect the outcome of her relationship. Tears collect in her eyes. She sits on the kitchen floor and calls Allison.

"Did you disappear, girl?" Allison answers her phone with a question.

"It's over. Will you help me move out?" Mary Ann cries uncontrollably.

"I'll be right there."

Mary Ann throws the roses out the window and starts packing all she can into some of her bags. Allison arrives just before Zac. He enters to find Mary Ann kissing Jake, saying good-bye. "What's going on?" he asks, semirelieved.

"We will talk later. I am moving out," Mary Ann says with tears.

Allison hugs Zac, apologizing. She knows this was great, and she feels terrible about the possibility that she provoked their breakup. Zac grabs Jake's leash, ties it to his collar, and exits with his little guy, leaving them to their task. The last thing he wants is this breakup, but he certainly wants no part of pressuring her while she is so emotionally distraught. He still remains the "great guy" without trying.

CHAPTER 7

Salt

*T*he weekend breakup hits Zac hard. He questions how things crashed and burned so quickly. Did he do something? Why wouldn't she tell him what was going on or how this happened? The apartment is now Zac and Jake's. She left her chair. Why? He did buy it for her, and she loved it. What was that about? Now Jake makes full claim to the chair, sitting on its back viewing the world from the window.

Monday arrives to a clear absence. Zac decides to take Jake to work with him. At work, Amanda, his boss and owner of the publishing company, walks past his office and notices a new face.

"Who's this little guy?" she asks, leaning into his office. Jake sits with perked ears, clearly investigating this new woman.

"This is Jake. I hope you don't mind that I brought him to work. He will be a good boy."

"A good boy, huh? Are you a good boy, Jake?" she asks. Jake sits still, with insecure interest. "OK, as long as he is a good boy, he can come to work," she says, smiling as she retreats toward her office.

The morning is still young, and Zac is caught up reviewing a thriller spy book when Amanda returns.

"So what's up? Why did you bring Jake in today?" she asks, leaning one hip on the doorframe and crossing her arms over her stomach.

He pulls himself away from his computer and twists his chair to look at her. "My girlfriend and I broke up over the weekend. I thought bringing him along would help us both," he replies with relative confidence.

"Oh, that sucks. Are you OK?" she asks, not overly concerned.

"Yeah, shit happens."

"What happened?"

"I don't know. I wish I did. She wouldn't talk about it." He is getting annoyed by her interrogation.

"Are you going to try to get her back?" Amanda continues the inquisition.

"Not thinking about it right now. I don't know. We haven't talked. I guess I will just wait and see what happens."

"Maybe you need to get in touch with your feminine side," she states abruptly.

Zac's annoyance is now changing colors. "I'll write that down," he responds rudely.

This increases Amanda's vigor. "I got just the thing for you," she says sarcastically.

"Now what? You have a friend you want to set me up with? Not now."

"Oh no, I like my friends." The banter continues. "I want you to start reviewing love stories. Clear the others. From now until further notice, you get the pleasure of reviewing and editing love stories. I am sure that will help you through a breakup. Who knows—maybe I will bring you a tub of ice cream," she says with pleasure.

"Really, I don't want that shit. Come on," Zac pleads.

"Too bad. What's your favorite flavor?"

"Brunettes," he says to her retreating back.

Zac is completely frustrated now. His recent breakup and fresh wounds will now have the salt of love stories aggressively rubbed in. He clears the exciting thrillers, intrigue, and action books from his schedule, knowing after lunch his slate will be salty. He calls Adan, and they agree to meet for lunch.

Walking into a sandwich shop with Jake in one arm, he notices a woman approaching the entrance. He opens and holds the door for her. She walks through and looks back in response. "Don't you think I can do it for myself, or did you just want a look at my ass?" she rudely questions. Shell-shocked by her response to his chivalry, he says nothing and scans the room for Adan. Finding Adan by the front window, he takes a seat, trying to hide Jake in his lap.

"What was that about?" Adan asks.

"How the fuck do I know? Maybe she is on her period," Zac replies dismissively. They order lunch with Jake in his lap. After lunch arrives Zac feeds Jake bits of meat from his turkey sandwich.

"You OK?" Adan asks, concerned.

"Yeah, I guess."

"You sound a little down. You need anything?" Adan asks.

"A noose for my boss." Zac's frustration lets loose.

"What?" Adan laughs.

"Amanda assigned me to love stories after I told her about the breakup. She said maybe I should get in touch with my feminine side. What the fuck?" Zac relates with anger.

"Did you tell her that your feminine side means the woman next to you in bed?" Adan laughs at his joke.

"Feminine side—have you ever heard a guy ask a woman to get in touch with her masculine side? What the fuck is that all about?" Zac continues the venting while feeding a hidden Jake.

"Sounds like she is some kind of feminist?" Adan questions.

"You think? I will bet money she has signed the emasculation proclamation. Maybe she wrote it. When did women decide that their quest for equality should be a war for superiority?" Zac is now rather livid at Amanda for rubbing the breakup in his face. "I was born a man and should not spend my life apologizing or getting in touch with my feminine side. I think that is part of relationship issues today. Couples get together; then the man accepts the proclamation, starts becoming less manly, then boom. The woman then wants to know what happened to her man. He's not the same man he used to be. Duh."

Zac's venting is now losing control, and Adan sits on his words as Zac continues his tirade.

"Hasn't their cause become hypocritical? If they deem men's superiority wrong, then wouldn't women's superiority be equally as wrong? This is about equality, and I have absolutely no problems with it. That is not what it is anymore, and it pisses me off." Zac's face reddens.

"Tell me really how you feel about this." Adan chooses words to lighten the mood, pretending to be getting in touch with his feminine side, while Zac pierces him with his eyes. "I like equality. It means women get on top half the time." Adan laughs at his joke.

"No. For you, it means you get on top half the time. You already make them do all the work." Zac laughs with Adan, slowing his rant.

"So Amanda got you worked up. You know she is A*mand*a." Adan laughs, thinking he is oh so clever. Zac shakes his head, wondering how Adan ever graduated junior high school.

Zac returns to his office with Jake to find Amanda was not joking. Not only has she loaded him up with love stories, a gallon of chocolate ice cream is melting on his desk.

This week drags, with Zac hating the new assignments. Jake clings to Zac, and Zac likes that they are inseparable, and he chooses some solitude for a couple of weeks. Zac and Jake's time together has become special, with Zac realizing Jake is more than just a dog—he's a friend.

Zac is home with Jake peering out the window on his chair when Adan calls.

"Dude, you ready to get out yet?"

Zac pauses, thinking about it. "Yeah, I am," he replies to Adan, realizing it's time he experiences some company other than Jake's.

"Good. You know what women say. The best way to get over your last is to get under your next. Well, I think the best way for you is to get over your next. Time for some sport fucking."

"All right, I'll meet you at the Blue Soul in an hour."

At the Blue Soul, Adan, Zac, and Derek sit at the bar. Zac discusses his breakup with Thomas, who offers Zac a night of free cocktails, which he readily accepts. Adan has attracted a woman and is offering to buy her panty droppers, a drink from the '80s that he overheard Derek ordering without a woman around. Derek sees Mary Ann's friends Ashley and Brenda, whom they met through Allison and Mary Ann. He tracks them down and interests them in cocktails with him and Zac, while Adan and his attraction separate themselves to a table.

"You remember Brenda and Ashley, don't you?" Derek asks Zac.

"Of course. How are you two tonight?"

"Good. Fine," they reply, obviously many cocktails into the night.

"Derek offered us drinks. I hope you don't mind," Brenda asks Zac.

"Not at all. Please join us. What would you two like?" Zac offers politely.

"Do you guys want to do some shots?" Ashley asks.

"Yes. Yes, we would," Derek answers without Zac's approval. Four shots are ordered, and they proceed to shoot them.

"I am sure that will help," Brenda tells Zac.

"Help what?" he asks.

"Mary Ann has a new boyfriend."

CHAPTER 8

Women

While Zac gets ready for another Friday night out with the guys, Jake climbs in his chair, avoiding dinner. Jake is a little tired from his "work" days, Zac thinks.

"Tired, buddy?" he asks as Jake lays his head down, ready for a nap. "All right," Zac says as he enters the bedroom. After a shower and change of clothes, Zac notices Jake is fast asleep. Leaving the light on for him, he departs to meet Adan and Derek at the Blue Soul.

Zac enters the Blue Soul and spots Derek, with his "style," dancing with a confused woman. Zac finds a table just off the dance floor and takes a seat. He can't help but chuckle a little watching Derek. Adan arrives and takes a seat next to Zac.

"What are we going to do with him?" Adan asks.

"Nothing, he continues to make us look good. Why fuck it up?"

The music breaks, and the woman, clearly embarrassed, walks swiftly away. Derek takes a seat at their table, thinking he is the new Casanova.

"What's up, guys?" he asks them.

"Just watching the show." Adan grins.

"There are a few hotties here. Going to get some tonight," Derek says with the utmost confidence.

Zac and Adan laugh hard as the cocktail waitress arrives. "What can I get you guys?" she asks.

Derek quickly responds, "I will have a piña colada. What about you guys?"

A shocked Adan says, "Cancel that. No fucking way will I be sitting here while you suck a piña colada through a straw. Three shots of tequila—we'll start with that."

"OK, guys." She walks off to collect the order.

"Can you believe that shit?" Adan says to Zac, questioning Derek's request.

"Of course I can," he says as he notices two ladies who just walked in wearing classic little black dresses. The women choose the table next to them, primping, fluffing their hair, sitting back, and crossing their legs.

Zac thinks this will be far too easy. Derek becomes excited, thinking one of them is his. Adan notices Derek and Zac looking past him and turns to see what is catching their attention.

Shit, he thinks as he recognizes one of the women. Too late, they have seen each other.

"Hi, Sandra," he says uncomfortably. A month ago, they'd had a fling for a few weeks.

"It's good to see you, Adan," she says without regret.

"You too," he says and turns back to Derek and Zac.

"Who is that?" Derek asks.

"You remember the woman taking all my time a few weeks ago?"

"Yeah," Zac replies as three shots of tequila are placed on the table.

"That's her."

"No shit," Derek says.

Zac takes a look at her friend and asks Adan who she is.

"I don't know. A friend, I guess." The three of them toast a traditional "cheers" and slam the shots. Both Sandra and her friend are watching.

"Which one do I get?" Derek questions.

Zac laughs. "Neither."

Sandra and her friend order two shots of tequila. Zac starts to think they are mirroring them. A sign of interest—a fact he is aware of due to his recent employment assignments.

"Would you ladies care to join us?" he asks and then realizes he probably should have checked with Adan first. Adan looks at him with a "whatever" look, not disappointed but not enthused.

"Sure," they reply and move their chairs between Adan and Zac, with Derek directly across from them. Sandra sits next to Adan and introduces Kelly to the three men.

The waitress returns, asking if they would care for more drinks. "A pink squirrel, and whatever the ladies would prefer," Derek states, thinking he is now the ladies' man.

"Certainly not that." Kelly laughs in disbelief.

"What the fuck?" Adan says. "Fine, bring him that shit. We will continue with four more shots." The four of them laugh, having not even heard of a pink squirrel. After the drinks arrive, the four commit the shots to memory while Derek stirs his sweet drink. As he takes a drink through the straw, Adan and Zac decide to save the two women from him and ask them to dance.

After many more drinks, lots of flirting and conversation, and quite a bit more dancing, Adan decides to a rerun with Sandra as the clock approaches midnight. They did have great sex. They just did not like each other. Zac and Kelly have been stuck together all night in obvious physical attraction.

As Adan announces his and Sandra's departure, Derek scans the room looking for a dance partner. Zac thinks this is going to be awkward—sitting with Derek—and asks Kelly if she would like to get out of there. She nods and stands up.

As Zac and Kelly walk down the street, he asks where she would like to go, thinking perhaps food or another bar might keep the night going.

"Your place," she says quickly.

"I am not that easy," he says jokingly.

"We will find out," she says with a smile and slips her arm around his.

They arrive at his apartment, kissing and groping each other wildly. Jake, now awake, is excited but wonders who this woman is. As he is ignored he just watches as they begin to shed their clothes. Zac and Kelly jump into bed, sexually attacking each other. A confused Jake walks to the bedroom and watches. That's what Mary Ann and Zac used to do, he thinks. He watches as they continue their passion.

After a few minutes, Jake walks unnoticed over to where Kelly dropped her shoes and takes one into the living room, where he begins to chew her black Prada heel.

Kelly wakes and begins seeking her clothes. Zac, awake in bed, decides to just lie there. "Would you like some breakfast?" he asks, hoping she doesn't.

"Thank you, but I should be going. Have you seen my other shoe?" she asks as she slips one on.

"No, but it has to be around here somewhere."

She continues her search with one shoe on, bouncing around the bedroom. Not finding it, she moves to the living room and spots Jake—full of pride with his accomplishment, one paw holding down his prey—facing away from her.

"What the fuck? You little asshole," she yells.

Zac, startled, asks, "What happened?"

"Your little fucker stole my shoe and ate half of it."

Zac stumbles into the living room. "Oh shit, what did you do?" he asks, giggling inwardly. Jake, with all of the pride of his accomplishment, lifts his butt into the air—in the familiar downward-facing-dog yoga position—and lifts his tail, his butt facing Kelly.

"Did that little shit just tell me to kiss his ass?" Full of anger, she yells at Zac.

Zac tries to remain calm but finds this both funny and costly at the same time. "I will buy you some new shoes," he says, holding his hands up.

"You are fucking right you will. You better call me and let me know when. Where is your phone?" She looks around the room, an angry glare in her eyes.

"On the counter top."

She grabs it and calls her own phone. "I have your number now. I expect new shoes by the end of the week." She takes off her other shoe and throws it into the living room in front of Jake and storms out the door, barefoot and pissed.

"Thanks, buddy, I really needed that first thing in the morning."

Jake walks to the leash, needing to take care of business.

"Give me a minute."

After Jake takes care of his business, they walk around the sidewalk bordering the park. Zac is a little hungover and decides to go with the flow. Along the sidewalk, Zac spots a new blue Honda with a round sticker on the bottom middle of the rear window that says, "I love my Border Terrier," and has a picture of the dog, centered. "Look, Jake, they love their Border Terrier too!" Jake jumps toward Zac in a circle. Suddenly he slows and starts sniffing by the car's driver's side door.

"No, don't do it," Zac tells Jake, thinking he is either going to take a shit or piss right by the car. Jake sits by the driver's door, looking up at Zac with shy eyes.

"Let's go," he tells Jake. Jake sadly looks down, and Zac picks him up. "What's wrong?" he asks. Jake just looks at him as they walk away. Back at the apartment, Zac feeds Jake and takes a nap on the couch. Jake looks at the one and a half shoes and ignores them, climbs onto his chair, and proceeds to watch the world outside.

Zac's life begins to take on a tone of monotony as another typical week passes, and again it's Friday night. "Another Friday night with the guys," Zac tells Jake after a walk. Then he readies himself for the night, deciding he'll dress up a bit more than usual and wear a sports coat over his teal button-down dress shirt. Jake climbs to his perch to scope the public. Zac walks to Jake, picks him up, gives him a big kiss, and sets him back on the chair.

Zac and Adan arrive at the Blue Soul at the same time. They enter, wondering where Derek could be. Looking over at the bar, Adan asks Thomas if Derek has arrived.

"Not yet—haven't seen him," he replies. They sit at the bar, looking around for both women and Derek.

"What are you guys having?" Thomas asks.

"Let's go with martinis tonight—got a little fucked up on tequila shots last week," Zac says.

"Any kind in particular?"

"Any kind will work," Adan says.

Thomas returns with the shaker and pours both martinis. Derek calls Adan's phone. "Wonder what this is about?" Adan asks Zac as he answers.

"Where are you?" Derek asks.

"At the Blue Soul, where did you think?"

"Good, I will be there in a few minutes."

Adan just hangs up without responding. He looks at Zac and informs him of Derek's pending arrival.

Thomas asks, "What's up with Derek?"

"What do you mean?" Zac grins at Adan in response to Thomas.

"Well, his dancing is a little, um, off, if you know what I mean."

"Yeah, he's a character, but he is pretty," Adan jokes as they all start laughing.

Derek enters with three women. One is older, and the other two are about Derek's age. He says, "Guys, let's get a table," and he leads the women to a table next to the dance floor.

"What the fuck is this?" Adan asks Zac.

Zac looks at Derek and the women taking seats at the table, and then he looks at Adan and says, "Interesting, for sure. Let's find out."

They pick up their martinis and direct themselves to the table with Derek and the three women. Derek proudly introduces Dora, Stephanie, and Julie—his mother, sister, and sister's friend, respectively.

Adan leans over to Zac and whispers, "Fucking kidding me."

Derek spies a cocktail waitress and requests her presence. "What can I get you?" she asks.

"I will have a Tom Collins," Dora says.

Derek requests a daiquiri, and Julie and Stephanie both ask for martinis.

Adan again leans to Zac. "You're fucking kidding me."

"At least those two ordered martinis," Zac responds, laughing along with Adan.

The music is on, and dancing is alive in the Blue Soul. Derek asks his mother to dance, and Zac and Adan just shake their heads in shock and decide to engage with Julie and Stephanie.

Dora dances proudly with her son, matching his slip-and-slide style. Derek looks back at the table and sees Julie and Stephanie watching with certain shame.

"Isn't he good?" Adan laughs as he asks the table.

Immediately, Zac backhands Adan's shoulder, trying to save the situation. Julie and Stephanie return their attention to Zac and Adan, avoiding the responsibility of answering. When Derek and his mother return, Adan and Zac immediately ask Stephanie and Julie to dance.

Adan wonders what to do as he dances with his friend's sister. Zac thanks God he is not dancing with Derek's sister.

Zac and Julie monopolize each other's attention throughout the night, while Adan's quandary becomes less relevant as they all consume more alcohol. Derek and his mother continue the outdated drink menu, trying to one-up each other with cocktails that Thomas finally refuses to make.

Dora decides the evening is over and asks Derek to take her home.

"OK, girls, we are leaving now," Derek says.

"Go ahead and take Mom home. Julie and I would like to stay awhile," Stephanie says, looking at her mother for approval.

"You guys have fun," Dora says as she grabs Derek's arm, wanting him to escort her out.

Derek looks at Adan and asks innocently, "Can I count on you to take care of my sister?"

"You certainly can," he replies with a devious grin. Derek proudly escorts his mother out the door.

"Finally," Stephanie exhales. "Now we can have some fun."

Zac and Adan look at each other—these two women are now ready to cut loose.

"Well, it's approaching midnight. You know nothing good happens after midnight," Adan tells the two women.

Julie looks at Zac. "Maybe you two need to hang out with a different crowd." She winks at him.

Before either can respond, Stephanie grabs Adan's hand. "Let's get out of here."

A stunned Adan asks, "What did you have in mind?"

"It's not what I have *in* mind. It is what I want *in* me," she informs him. As she begins to drag him out, he smiles relentlessly.

"Oh shit," Zac says, watching this episode. He turns to look at Julie as she stands, looking at him.

"What the fuck are you waiting for?" she asks. Zac stands, and they all depart.

Julie and Zac arrive at his apartment, with Jake again perplexed about another woman. Julie strips to nothing quickly and rips Zac's clothes off. Jake wonders if Zac is being attacked but does nothing. Zac is being attacked quite to his pleasure.

Zac and Julie hit the bed aggressively, writhing in Julie's sexual conquest with the abandon of all senses. Jake walks to the bedroom. Both of them are locked in the famously pleasurable sixty-nine position.

Jake just sits, watching. Well I guess they can't lick their own, so I guess they lick each other's, he thinks. He then searches the room for bounty. He finds her panties and begins to roll around on them. He sits up, looks down at the panties, and picks them up in his mouth. What is that taste? he thinks. He proceeds to the bathroom and stands on his rear legs, balancing his front paws on the toilet. He then drops the panties in the toilet. Jake returns to the living room, spreads out on the floor, and falls asleep.

After the conclusion of their desires, Julie heads to the bathroom. Unaware of her panty situation, she sits on the toilet, pees, and flushes.

Julie wakes in the morning next to Zac. She stretches as Zac contemplates not only how he was aggressively and willingly taken, but more importantly, what happened with Adan and Stephanie. This could be a problem for Derek. He turns his head toward Julie and offers to make breakfast.

She sits up, saying, "I can't, sorry. I have to get home to my wife. Have you seen my panties?" she asks.

"What did you just say?" Zac freaks out.

"I need to get home to my wife, Stephanie. Do you know where my panties are?" She responds as if this is a normal event for her.

"Stephanie is your wife? You guys are married? Oh shit." He lies back in bed, completely blown away.

"Excuse me, do you know where my panties are?" she asks again.

"No, I don't. Lock the door on the way out." He rolls over.

"I need my panties," she says.

"Apparently, you don't," Zac replies, hoping she will leave soon.

Jake, now sitting atop his chair, watches Julie leave. He then jumps off the chair, runs straight to the bedroom, and jumps on the bed. He looks at Zac with shame.

"I don't know, OK? Leave me alone." Jake lays his head down, looking at Zac as they both fall asleep.

CHAPTER 9

Real

Jake and Zac wake up a couple of hours later. After Jake's walk, Zac starts questioning what happened the night before. He decides to call Adan to see if he is as shocked.

"What a night," Adan answers his phone.

"Yeah, I am confused," Zac replies.

"Yeah, well, I really like Stephanie. She is so hot," Adan says with excitement.

"Dude, what did she tell you? Is she still with you?" Zac asks, confused.

"No, she left early. We had a great night. Hot sex—even a little crazy. I guess I have to figure out how to tell Derek though. How did it go with Julie?"

"It was hot and crazy too, but this morning I asked if she wanted breakfast. She refused, telling me she had to get home to her wife."

"What did you say? Did you say her wife?"

"Yeah, dude, her *wife*!"

"That's some crazy shit. She is married to a woman?" Adan freaks a little.

"Wait, do you know who Julie's wife is?" Zac asks, realizing Adan probably has no clue.

"No, I wasn't with her. You were."

"Yeah, well, you were with her wife last night."

"What? You mean Julie and Stephanie are married?"

"Yeah, dude. When I asked her about breakfast, she said she had to get home to her wife, Stephanie."

The phone is silent for a bit. Adan, second-guessing himself, asks, "Dude, did you use a condom?"

"No, she said she was on the pill. What about you?"

"Stephanie told me the same." Another silence captures the conversation. Both know what the consequences of this could be. "Oh fuck. What the fuck is this about?" Adan says with fear.

"You know what this is about. We know better. What the fuck were we thinking?" Zac resigns himself to the situation.

"Zac, they both hit us quick after Derek and his mom left." A confused Adan tries to put the pieces together.

"You think? As soon as they were gone, these girls both got crazy aggressive. This is crazy, dude. I got to go. I will talk to you this week." Zac wonders what to do next.

"Wait." Adan clings to the conversation. "We just got a couple of hot lesbians," he says, excited, like this was some form of conquest.

"We will see if you feel the same if you need a minivan in nine months," Zac abruptly tells him. "Later dude." Zac hangs up the phone. "I can't fucking believe this," he says out loud as Jake looks up from his perch. "I know, I know." He looks at Jake with a rush of anxiety.

Monday comes without much excitement due to the weekend worries. Jake and Zac get to the office, and Zac turns on his computer. Jake sits in the corner behind Zac's left shoulder. Zac is worried about the outcome of Friday night. "What do I do?" he asks Jake. Jake turns and runs out of the office. Yeah, running does sound like the best defense, he thinks.

Jake decides to see who is in the offices. Walking down the hall he enters the first door to the left. This is the office adjacent to Zac's. No one is in. Jake looks around. What can I get away with? he thinks. He walks to the threshold, lifts his leg, and marks his territory. Jake leaves, off to find the next office. He marks two more thresholds along the hall, until he enters Amanda's office. "Hi, Jake," she tells him. He sits by the doorway, disappointed. This is the threshold he really wanted to pee on. Oh well, I will get her later, he thinks. He turns, leaves her office, walks down the hall to the front of Zac's office, and lies down right in the doorway. He wants to see everyone's reaction as they enter their respective offices.

Zac is completely unaware of Jake's peeing adventure. His phone rings—it's Adan.

"Dude, I am freaking out. Derek called and asked how it went Friday night."

"What did you say?" Zac wonders how bad this could get.

"I told him I was busy and I will get back to him."

Zac takes a breath. "Do we need to tell him what happened? His sister is married to Julie. He probably would not believe us anyway. I mean, really, why cause shit when he is not going to believe it? If we tell him the truth, then he will ask Stephanie, or both of them, and this could develop into some shit. Think about it. We tell him the truth, and he does not believe us. Then he tells his mom. Then he and his mom ask them. They could both lie about it and say they went home right after they left. Then we look like idiots and liars. What if they tell the truth? Then Derek is pissed at us, and so is his mother. Stephanie and Julie are then in a weird spot with Derek and Dora. What happens when they question them about what they did? More importantly, why?" Zac is trying to calm down Adan.

"Yeah, you're right. Why didn't Derek tell us that they were together? That makes me wonder what the fuck is up. Does he even know they are together, and if so—oh shit," he says. "Do you think this was planned? Do you think Derek set this up?"

Zac sits back in his chair, looking up at the ceiling. "We just have to play this slow. Keep the conversation light. You know, ask Derek if Stephanie and Julie had a good night. We need to prod a little without giving anything up. See if we can get anything out of him without saying anything. You know what? I will call Derek. You just avoid him until I call you back. I will call him this week. I am busy now and have to get back to work. OK?" asks Zac.

"Yeah, that's good. Cool. I will talk to you later."

Meanwhile, Jake is observing staff members coming to work and sniffing the air.

Air-freshening spray is brought out and sprayed up and down the hall. Jake just sits there, panting with his tongue hanging out and a slight smile on his face.

After work, Zac thinks he should call Derek. He wonders how to bring this up, what to ask, and how to respond to whatever Derek says. He formulates his plan and decides to heed his advice to Adan and keep it light, with some probing for information.

He dials Derek's number. It rings as he thinks about the situation.

"Zac, how are you?" Derek asks.

"Good. How are you, and how is your lovely mother?" Zac asks, trying to deflect the situation so he can control the conversation.

"She is great."

"So, Derek, did Stephanie and Julie have a good time Friday night?"

"Yes, they did, and I want to thank you and Adan for taking care of them."

What the fuck does he mean? Zac thinks as panic sets in. Zac decides not to push this and to avoid showing his hand. "Good, I am glad they had fun. I am sure you and your mother arrived home safe."

"Yes, we did. It was a lovely night, wouldn't you agree?" Derek asks all too kindly.

Is he fucking with me? Zac thinks. "Yes, it was, and I was glad to meet your sister and Julie. Please give them my regards." He hopes to get some minor bit of information at this point.

"I will. Perhaps we can do it again sometime?" Derek asks.

"Possibly," Zac replies, knowing there is no way in hell he wants to see them again.

"Have a good week. Are we going out this weekend?" Derek asks.

"We'll see. I have a busy week, and I think I need a weekend off. You have a good week also, and we will talk later."

At work late Wednesday morning, Jake decides this place needs some enlightening. He leaves Zac's office and strolls to the restrooms to the right of Zac's office. At the door of the men's room, he turns to scope the area. No one is looking, so he pushes the unlocked swinging doors to the men's restroom and enters. In the corner by the two stalls sits a basket, on top of a stool, holding unwrapped toilet-paper rolls. Perfect, he thinks. Then he grabs one with his teeth and turns toward the door. How do I get out? he thinks.

He hears the toilet flush in the furthest stall, and he rushes under the closest stall divider and hides in the stall. He was unaware of anyone, due to poor reconnaissance. Shoes click as the gentleman walks to the door. The gentleman opens the door to exit, and Jake darts to make his escape with the coveted toilet paper. That was close, he thinks.

Strutting down the hall with his captured toilet paper, he targets the first doorway where he marked his territory two days prior. Doing this, he passes Zac's office very quickly, hoping not to be seen. Now at the doorway, he places the roll on the very spot where he had peed. See if they get it, he thinks and then heads back to the restroom for more.

The second capture goes as the first. However, he has to wait until someone enters the restroom before his escape is possible. The third, however, is a debacle. Following the previously proven procedure, he escapes the restroom to find the first office owner standing in the hall, wondering what this means. Jake has not been seen yet. Uh oh. What to do? Where can I hide? He turns around and steps in front of the restroom.

Amanda exits the adjacent women's restroom at this exact time and looks down at the guilty Jake. "What are you doing?" she asks as Jake sits down, looking up at her with the freshly stolen toilet paper in his mouth. Realizing he has been caught, he plays the cute dog with the puppy eyes everyone seems to love. "You are a funny little guy, aren't you? Give it up." She reaches down to retrieve the toilet paper. He drops it and stares up at her. "Don't give me that. Now get back to your office."

At Zac's office door, Jake greets his friend with a bark.

"What did you do?" Zac asks sternly but in jest, not really caring, just wanting to show control in front of Amanda. Jake lowers his head and walks to his corner and lies down. He decides to wait a few days for his next office adventure.

Friday afternoon arrives, and Zac and Jake are at work after lunch. Jake is feeling rather lively and decides today is a good day for an offensive operation. He walks to the doorway of Zac's office and scans up and down the hallway. He sneaks down the hallway to Amanda's office. What could this be? he thinks. She has taken her shoes off, and they are just to the side of the desk. Amanda is on the phone, leaning back in her chair, seemingly very occupied. Jake sneaks to the first shoe quietly. I got it, he thinks. He grabs her shoe by its heel and sneaks backward out of her office with his eyes on her the whole way. He manages to make the escape. He turns in the hall and beelines proudly down to Zac's office and hides in his corner.

"What did you do?" asks Zac. "You know she is going to be pissed. But let's see how long this takes her to notice." He starts giggling.

An hour later Zac hears Amanda approaching his office. "Does Jake have something that doesn't belong to him?" she asks prior to entering. Zac looks at Jake and the shoe in front of him and says nothing.

She turns the corner and enters his office. "Jake, what did you do?" she asks, and still Zac remains quiet. Jake looks at the shoe. Amanda starts toward the shoe. Jake stands immediately, protecting his catch. "Give it up!" she commands. Jake lifts his leg and pees all over the shoe and into the toe of the shoe.

"What the fuck? You little shit! Zac, that's it. Take the rest of the day off. Take your little heathen home, and don't bring him back. He can't be in the office anymore." Jake sits down now, completely disinterested in her shoe, and looks up to Zac.

"OK. You did it now," he says first to Amanda, then to Jake. Zac's mind is occupied with greater concerns, and taking the rest of the afternoon off sounds like a blessing.

Zac takes Jake home. He has not retired his work attire yet and decides a beer sounds good right about now. He has already decided a Friday night off is the plan and looks forward to it. Zac finds the necessary beer glass. His preference is a typical pint glass, small base opening to a larger mouth. Zac sits on the couch and pours the beer. Jake jumps off the chair and darts to his food dish. "Hungry, are you?" Zac asks. Jake licks his lips as his answer. "Just a minute." Zac goes to the bathroom to drop a dump.

Jake starts looking at the freshly poured beer. Why does he like that, and why don't I ever get some? he thinks. Curiosity sets into Jake. He walks to the coffee table the beer is on, jumps onto the couch, and then steps across onto the table. Looking into the full glass directly below, he starts to drink the beer. Different, he thinks. Halfway down the glass, his head no longer fits. He sits down on the table, looks at the remainder, and lets out a fabulous burp. As he gets dizzy he realizes it was filling and climbs back onto his chair.

Zac returns from the bathroom to find Jake on the chair. "You still hungry?" he asks. Jake barely looks at him and does nothing. "OK." Zac sits down and reaches for his beer. Did he drink some before the bathroom? He isn't sure. Deciding he already had some, he takes a drink and turns on the television.

Zac notices Jake's head sort of swerves upward when Jake hears the sounds from the television. Jake turns to look at Zac with double vision. He has no idea what's happening. Tongue hanging out and beginning to pant, he just stares at Zac. "You OK?" Zac asks.

Jake has obtained his first drunk. Jake, still staring at Zac, begins to slide toward the backside of the chair. Unable to control his motor skills, he slips until he falls off the back of the chair with a thud.

"What the—you OK, Jake? What's going on?"

Jake appears from behind the chair, looking at Zac. His face is grizzled, tongue stuck between his teeth, and he has droopy eyes. He is completely unhappy with his current condition. He begins to walk toward Zac, stumbling along the way.

Zac looks at him, completely puzzled. "What are you doing?" Jake walks to Zac's feet and leans on Zac's leg with his back to the couch. His head is wobbly, and just about everything is out of control at this point. He tries to look up at Zac but can't manage it. His head beginning to droop, he feels it. He vomits all over Zac's shoes.

"What the fuck is it with you and shoes?" Zac asks while he pulls his feet away. Jake turns away and stumbles to the middle of the living room and passes out. Taking his now beer-vomit-smelling shoes off, Zac says out loud, "That little fucker drank half my beer." After the removal of his shoes, he picks up Jake to make sure he is OK. He takes him to bed and places him by the pillows to sleep it off.

CHAPTER 10

Escape

*S*itting on his favorite spot atop his chair with the sun warming him, Jake hears the keys unlocking the door. Perking his ears, he looks over his left shoulder to greet Zac. The door opens. What? What is this? Mary Ann and Zac both enter. Jake's heart races with excitement and happiness, and he jumps off the top of the chair, landing two feet from Mary Ann, and leaps up into her arms. His tail is not wagging—his whole body is shaking as he starts kissing her with the hunger of his love. Finally, I got her back, he thinks. Mary Ann is giggling and kissing him, while Zac smiles and hugs both of them with Jake in the middle.

Jake could not be happier. She better not put me down, he thinks as she carries him to the chair and sits. Jake starts whining. He rolls over to his back and begs her to give up the TLC. She rubs his belly gladly, while he tries to control himself.

Zac is full of smiles as he watches the two of them reconnect. Mary Ann's baby talk fills the room, while Jake keeps an eye on her. She better not leave, he thinks.

Zac asks Jake if they should go for a walk. Of course, Jake thinks, could it be the three of us together again? He jumps off Mary Ann, beelines to the leash by the door, and starts jumping in circles. Zac grabs the leash off of the hook and bends down to attach it to his collar. Jake backs up toward Mary Ann. Oh no, I want her to do it, he thinks. Zac and Mary Ann both smile as Zac hands her the leash. She bends over and attaches it to Jake's collar. Finally, I got her on my leash, he thinks. They leave the apartment, Jake proud, excited, exhilarated, happy, and relieved. Zac finally got it, he thinks.

Now on the sidewalk, Jake walks ahead, with Mary Ann holding the leash. Look what I got, he gloats to anyone and anything he sees. Still in disbelief, he looks back every few steps to make sure he still has her. Mary Ann and Zac are holding hands as he walks them. The trio walk around a couple of blocks, with Jake marking his territory at every chance. She's mine. He's mine. And this is my territory.

After the walk, back in the apartment, it's dinnertime. Zac reaches for Jake's food and bends to his dish. Oh no, you don't, thinks Jake. Jake rushes to his food dish and stands with his left paw in it. He looks up at Zac with eyes that ask for Mary Ann to feed him.

"OK." Laughing, Zac calls to Mary Ann. "Check this out," he says, pointing to Jake. "I think he wants you to feed him." She grabs the box of food from Zac and looks down at Jake.

Yes!

She bends over toward the bowl. Jake steps out of the bowl and looks at her, not the food, as she pours it in his dish. He sits and begins happy whining. After filling the bowl, she stands, looking at him.

"Is that what you wanted?" Jake grabs her pant leg, toying with her in a playful yes. Jake attacks his food. After all, he is a little hungry from today's excitement.

After dinner, Zac and Mary Ann are snuggling on the couch watching television, tickling and teasing each other with giggles and affection. Oh no, not without me, Jake thinks. Jake jumps on them, landing between them on both laps. As all three face the television, he pushes himself up and backward toward them. One of his shoulder blades rests on the right side of Zac's ribs, and the other rests on the left side of Mary Ann's. He lifts his head, trying to see their faces above him at the same time. They both laugh as they start rubbing his belly. Could this get any better? Jake wonders. Maybe if I don't move, they will do this forever.

Zac gets up, goes to the kitchen, and retrieves two glasses and a couple bottles of beer. This disturbs Jake's comfort, so he jumps to the other side of Mary Ann and sits next to her, facing the television, and, behind it, the kitchen. Jake starts pawing at her with his left paw. We can hold hands again, he wishes. Mary Ann bends to her right, to Jake's level, and they kiss each other. She then offers her upturned palm. Jake places his paw in it and whines slightly with joy.

Zac walks back into the living room and sees the two holding hands (paws, to Jake). Jake sees him coming and stares at the television with his ears pinned back and a guilty-looking mug. I don't think he can see me. It will be OK; I will just be quiet, Jake thinks.

"Really? OK," Zac says, laughing in response. Jake does not acknowledge him. He does not want to ruin the moment. Zac sits and pours the beer into Mary Ann's glass, then his.

A couple hours later, Jake recognizes their rustling and knows it's time for bed. Jake jumps off the couch, takes a couple of right turns, and jumps up on the bed—straight for the pillows. I think they will let me sleep up here tonight, he wishes as he lies on the pillows. When Zac and Mary Ann walk in, Jake pretends to be asleep already.

"Yeah, right. Move your butt," she says in a teasing tone. OK, but it was worth a shot. He walks from the pillows to the foot of the bed and curls up in the middle, not moving again but following Mary Ann's every move with his eyes. Everyone now in bed, Jake saddens, slightly disappointed. I guess I will have to stay down here, he thinks.

"Jake, come on," Mary Ann calls as she pats the small vacancy between Zac and her. Thrilled, Jake wastes no time curling up between them.

Morning provides for snuggling with both Mary Ann and Zac. After breakfast, Jake sits under the hanging leash, staring at the door. He tries to ignore them but hopes they see him.

"OK," Mary Ann says happily as she reaches for the leash and removes it from its hook. She leans over and attaches the leash to his collar.

Here we go again! Jake thinks while Zac opens the door. Wait, I got her on my leash, but I need him on it too, Jake thinks and sits down.

"What are you doing?" she asks. Jake looks at Zac, and she hands him the leash. Jake now has Zac on the leash, but he wants them both on it. He looks down, disappointed.

"Let's go," Zac says, and Jake looks at Mary Ann.

"I just had the leash," she says as Zac reaches to give it back. Now the leash is back in Mary Ann's hand, and Jake looks at Zac. Both kneel down to Jake, seeking his problem. With the leash in Mary Ann's hand, Jake playfully bites Zac's hand and directs it to the leash.

"Fine," Zac says and takes the leash. No, no, you guys are not getting this, Jake thinks. He then bites Mary Ann's hand and directs it to the leash.

"He wants us both to walk him," she says. Jake jumps in acknowledgment of her statement.

"OK," Zac says as he reaches for the leash. This time they both hold the leash, to Jake's thrill.

Walking down the sidewalk, Jake is the proudest person on earth. I have both of them on my leash! He walks with his head high and proud. Prancing the blocks, Jake can't believe this. He finally has them back together.

Back at home, Jake climbs *his* chair and sits on its back, looking out the window and then back at Zac's and Mary Ann's every move. Mary Ann sits in *her* chair and opens a book. I am the happiest person on earth, he thinks. This is perfect. He begins to calm from the excitement of the last two days. Still fearful she might leave, he does not allow himself a nap as he continues to fight drowsiness. A few hours into her reading, Mary Ann falls asleep with the sun warming her like a blanket. Jake crawls off the back of the chair and moves onto the couch. I can keep an eye on her from here, he thinks, and I will just watch TV until she wakes.

Jake hears keys in the door as he wakes up on top of his chair. He turns to see who is entering. Zac walks into the room, looking at Jake.

"What's up, buddy?" he asks. Jake slowly rests his head on the chairback. Saddened, he realizes Zac is alone.

"Were you asleep?" Zac asks. Jake further saddens, realizing he has awakened from the best dream. He refuses to look at Zac.

Jake continues peering into the street. Across the street he sees a familiar person walking away with another woman. Jake lifts his head up, perking his ears. She turns her head to the left in comment to her friend. Is it? It is. Jake struggles to speak actual words. There she is. Jake stands on the chairback and begins barking to get her attention. She can't hear him, but he's going to do what he can. Zac comes into the living room.

"What's going on?" he asks. Jake looks at him and points to the street with his nose. "What is it?" Zac moves toward the window.

Mary Ann turns the corner and disappears from view just as Zac reaches the window and takes the view. Jake lies down on the chairback. Why can't Zac get it right?

"Jake, you want to go for a walk?" Zac asks. Jake remains on the chair, motionless. He ignores Zac for the remainder of the night.

Bedtime arrives, and Zac calls Jake to bed. Jake crawls off the chair and begins a slow walk into the bedroom. At the door to the bedroom, he looks up at Zac, turns, walks back to his chair, climbs into the seat, and curls up and falls asleep.

CHAPTER 11

Angst

After a few weeks of nothing notable, Zac decides it's time to get back out. Friday night arrives, and Derek and Adan are ready to get back to the Blue Soul.

Derek arrives after Adan and Zac in a vintage 1970s polyester suit. He is wearing light-brown pants with a matching vest, a jacket with a bright-gold huge-collared shirt, no tie, and purple suede shoes.

Adan sees him strutting in. "What the fuck?"

"I don't know, dude. At least he isn't boring," Zac responds.

Derek looks around for his friends. As he locates Zac and Adan, they try to cover their faces. "Guys, how's the scene? Any local talent available?" Derek inquires with such confidence.

"Yeah, there is a couple of women over in the corner that look like they are from the '70s," Zac says, laughing.

Adan busts up with laughter. "I am sure your suit will give them a facelift."

Even Derek cannot refuse laughing. "All right, all right," he concedes. "You guys know vintage is now in," Derek says, actually looking at the two women in the corner.

"You know the difference between vintage and classic, right?" Zac asks.

"Of course I do, and I just happen to pull off both tonight," Derek states confidently.

Silence. Zac and Adan smile and avoid laughing at Derek.

Zac and Adan are a little gun-shy after the wife episode and are reluctant to approach women tonight. Derek is enjoying his round of drinks, long forgotten, while Zac and Adan stick to martinis. Derek notices three women sitting at the bar, in discussion with Thomas.

Thomas is having fun loading them up with cocktails but can't decide which woman to devote his attention to. Derek sees this as a perfect opportunity. Thomas is getting them drunk, and Derek looks fabulous—at least, he thinks so. He steps away from the table and decides they are lucky to be with him tonight.

"Ladies," he says as he walks to the bar, "how are you this evening?"

Zac and Adan decide to watch the show.

"Fine," two of the three chime. The third looks him up and down, then at Thomas, and the two start laughing.

After an uncomfortable silence, Derek asks with a smile, "Perhaps you ladies would prefer to join my friends and me at our table?"

"Where are you sitting?" the third woman asks.

"Over there with my two friends." He points with his nose.

They look over at Zac and Adan. "Sure," the first two women agree.

The third elects to stay at the bar and continue conversing with Thomas. The other two grab their cocktails, and Derek escorts them to the table. Thomas lightly thanks Derek. Now the choice is made, and she made it.

As they sit down, Adan proceeds with introductions. "Ladies, this is Zac."

Zac says, "And this is Adan." They reach out for soft handshakes.

"I am Beth, and this is Andrea. It is nice to meet both of you." Derek reaches out to shake their hands. They politely oblige and turn their attention to Zac and Adan.

"What is up with your friend?" Beth asks Adan, referring to Derek.

"What do you mean?" he asks.

"He is so good-looking, but what are his clothes about? He looks trapped in a bad dream," she says.

"Well, he is certainly a character, and you have to admire his confidence. He is a great dancer. You should ask him to dance." He simply couldn't resist saying it, and he begins to giggle.

Zac looks at him with a grin, knowing if she does ask Derek, Adan could get slapped. No need to stop this.

Andrea asks Zac, "What is going on?"

"This should be good," he tells her. "Let's just see what happens."

"OK." She starts to lean into Zac, who intently watches Beth as he sips his martini.

"Would you like to dance?" Beth asks Derek.

"Well, of course," he says as he stands with his hand out.

The two begin dancing, and Derek doesn't disappoint—his personalized style of dancing.

Beth begins to wonder what is going on. He has no rhythm, and the gliding-sliding is throwing her off.

"Oh shit," Andrea says and starts laughing. Adan and Zac join the laughter. Halfway through the song, Beth stops and walks off the floor, straight to Adan. Zac has been anticipating this moment and smiles.

"Fucking asshole," she tells Adan as she passes and proceeds to the bar.

Feeling bad about the setup, he gets up and follows her, trying to apologize.

"That was funny," Andrea whispers to Zac as Derek sits down, perplexed.

"Would you care to dance?" Zac asks her.

Though insecure about what she just saw, she accepts.

Zac and Andrea spend the remainder of the night dancing and drinking. Adan tries to polish the turd he created with Beth. Derek decides to call it a night and departs alone yet another night. Adan runs out of luck with Beth as she remains at the bar with the third woman and Thomas.

Deciding he has spent too much pick-up equity, Adan leaves, watching Zac and Andrea getting closer. "Good for him," he says.

Making out at the table with Andrea, Zac decides it is time to get out of there. She agrees. As they walk out, he notices Thomas is now kissing both the women at the bar.

Thomas, noticing Zac and Andrea leaving, says, "Tell Derek double thanks for me."

"All right." Zac and Andrea leave, holding hands.

As the door to Zac's apartment opens, Jake perks up. They both walk in, and Jake's mood changes from excitement to angst. They start embracing passionately. Her Versace long-sleeve black dress falls to the floor as she pushes Zac to the bed. While they are entangled in passion, Jake recognizes opportunity. As the two persist into the night, Jake sneaks into the bedroom and steals her dress. Removing it to the living room, he begins shredding it with his teeth. After a couple hours of this, the dress resembles nothing but a pile of threads.

The two lie in bed together, and the time reaches three in the morning. Andrea decides the night is over.

"You can stay the night if you want," Zac says, this time actually hoping she will.

"I am not into sleepovers right now," she says.

"All right, if you insist," he states, staring at her.

She starts a search for her dress. "Where is my dress?" she asks, looking at Zac.

Oh shit. "You dropped it on the floor, didn't you?" he says, knowing Jake may have had his way with it. He turns a light on in the appearance of being cooperative. The dress is not in the bedroom. Zac gets out of bed and peers into the living room. "Fuck," he says as Jake jumps onto his chair. "What did you do?" he yells at Jake as Jake covers his eyes with his paws.

"What the fuck? That is a five-hundred-dollar dress. I just got it today," she says, quivering.

"It's OK. I will buy you another. I am sorry." Zac tries to calm her.

"What a fucked-up week," she says and starts crying.

"I am sorry. I will get you a new one," he says as he puts his arms around her.

"It doesn't matter." She continues crying.

"Are you OK?" he asks, realizing this episode might have triggered something else that has nothing to do with the dress.

"I had a fucked-up week. I am sorry for reacting like this." She continues crying.

"What happened?" he asks, recognizing he could have just opened a can of worms he wants no part of.

"I caught my boyfriend with another woman."

"Fuck, you have a boyfriend?" he asks with uncertainty.

"I had one. We broke up."

"I am sorry. Did you know the other woman?" he asks, saying all the wrong things.

"Yes, it was my bitch of a mother."

What do you do with this? he thinks. "I am sorry," he says again with all the uncertainty of the moment.

"I got to go, so give me some clothes to wear," she says with tears.

"What would you like?"

"Just some sweats or something."

He retrieves some sweat pants and a sweat shirt. She puts them on, then puts her four-inch heels on and leaves without words, completely distraught. Zac sits, stunned, thinking about the situations he has had with women lately. Jake jumps off the chair and lies on the threads of the dress, content with his conquest.

Another week passes with Zac pouring over love stories pathetically. Friday is here, and the typical night out is on the agenda. Zac is dressed and leaving his apartment when he notices Jake seems sad. Zac sits on the couch and calls Jake over. Jake jumps off his chair with the view and leaps up on Zac's lap. Zac stays awhile, giving Jake TLC, petting and rubbing his belly, and kissing him. Jake's mood appears to be up after a while, and Zac decides to meet the boys. Jake climbs back on the chair as Zac locks the door.

At the Blue Soul, Zac arrives to find Derek and Adan sitting at the bar, talking with Thomas. "What's up, guys?" Zac asks.

"Thomas was filling in the details of the threesome he had last week," an excited Adan states.

Derek, enthralled with the story, requires more. "How did it end?" he asks Thomas.

"Who asks that?" Thomas replies with a concerned look at Derek.

"We all know how it ended," Zac says.

"What can I get you?" Thomas asks Zac.

"I will stick with my martini, thanks." Thomas starts the martini when a stunning woman walks in alone. Her cobalt-blue dress with matching heels, long flowing auburn hair, and deep-green eyes captivate the four of them.

"You ever see her before?" Adan asks Thomas.

"Nope, but hope to see the rest of her." Thomas grins.

She selects a seat at a table and ignores the four men. "That's it. I am going in," an excited Derek says.

"Yeah, right. Don't fucking move. You aren't fucking this up for me." Adan stops Derek.

A little competition, Zac thinks.

While Derek, Adan, and Thomas eyeball her, Zac steps away from the bar and walks directly to her. "Hi," he says, looking down at her.

"Hi back," she says with sarcasm.

"I'm Zac," he says as he reaches out to shake her hand.

"I am not," she says as she shakes his hand.

"Good, I would hate to hit on another Zac," he says, thinking he is clever.

"How many have you hit on?" she says with a smile.

"Nice," he replies, smiling. "None, and I am glad I am not now."

"Are you going to stand there trying to look down my dress, or are you going to sit down, offer me a drink, and continue this banter?" She stuns him, physically and mentally.

"Sure, what would you care for?" he asks, pulling out a chair and winking at his friends at the bar.

"Are you asking about my drink preference, or is there hidden meaning?" She stares at him, smiling.

"Sure," he says, answering both as he sits.

She laughs. "I will have a martini." Zac looks over to the bar again and finds Thomas, Adan, and Derek with their jaws on the bar.

The ordered martini arrives. "My name is Constance, Zac." Her eyes stare firmly into his.

"Did you say Constance or constant?" he asks playfully.

"Sure," she replies, laughing.

Flirting conversation continues while Derek and Adan attempt their own seek-and-destroy missions.

"Would you care to dance?" Zac asks, thinking he could get his hands on her.

"No, I wouldn't. I would prefer you to sit closer to me. That is what you are trying to accomplish, aren't you?"

"If you insist, I can oblige," he says as he reaches over and pulls her chair closer to his.

"I guess that will work." She leans into him and kisses his cheek. They engage in more flirting, touching hands and arms, showing affection without kissing.

Adan seems to be having an off night, and after a solid crash and burn, he begins to wonder if his time would be better spent just conversing with Thomas. He sits at the bar and concedes the night.

Derek, however, is on a roll. His lack of dancing expertise this night has kept women in his court and him off the floor. Derek has attracted a sexy blonde that he is nervous around. He is having difficulty with not only conversation but actual speaking. He pardons himself momentarily and approaches Adan and Thomas.

"Guys, she asked me to leave," he explains while physically shaking.

"And?" Thomas asks.

"And do what?" Adan asks.

"She wants me to go back to her place and show her how to make a slow comfortable screw," he responds with discomfort.

"Wait. She actually said that?" Thomas giggles at him.

"Yes."

"Do you know how to make one?" Adan asks, laughing.

"No, I don't. Thomas, will you tell me how?" Derek asks with panic in his voice.

"Sure, I will teach you tomorrow, but you have to leave with her now," he says, laughing hard.

"Go," they both tell Derek.

"OK, but I still don't know how to make it," he says.

"We know. Now go, before she changes her mind," says Thomas forcefully.

Derek turns, walks to her, places her hand in his, and they leave.

"Can't wait to hear about this," Adan tells Thomas.

"Yeah," Thomas agrees, turning his attention to a woman at the bar.

"Zac, is there any other place you would like to be?" Constance asks.

"No, I am having a great time. Would you prefer to go to another place?" he asks, not aware of her intent.

"Actually, yes, there is another place I would like to be."

"I am happy to accommodate. Where would you like to go?" he asks politely.

"You know, Zac, I am a woman, not some girl. I know what I want and when I want it. Right now I have a strong desire to see what the ceiling in your bedroom looks like."

Oh shit. He stands and grabs her by the hand, and they escape the Blue Soul.

Hoping Jake is not going to stir the pot, Zac enters his apartment with Constance.

Jake, first excited Zac is home, then becomes territorial. They start toward the bedroom, as Jake leaps off his chair and beats them to the bed. He jumps on it and races to the pillows. Constance and Zac are feeling each other and kissing as they approach the bed. Jake growls to get their attention. They turn to see what the problem is as Jake curls his back and drops a sloppy dump on the pillow.

"What the fuck are you doing?" startled, Zac elevates his voice. Jake then turns to look at them and drags his butt across the sheets, wiping the leftovers.

"That kills it," she says.

"No, we can go to the couch." Zac tries to finish what she started.

"I don't think so. I can't fuck you the way I want on a couch. You know a lady on the streets, and now you will miss the sheets. Good night. Have fun jerking off over this." She turns and leaves the bedroom, then the apartment.

Dejected, Zac sits on the couch. Jake jumps up, looking for TLC. Zac can't refuse and rubs his belly.

"What's going on, Jake? You have fucked around with all the women I bring home." Jake perks his ears, looking up at Zac. "Should I go to their places from now on?" Jake's ears retract sadly. "What's the deal?" Jake turns over, sits up on Zac's lap, and kisses him. He then jumps back on his chair and lies down.

Derek calls the next morning, and Zac answers reluctantly. "What's up, Derek?"

"Zac, I am in love. I am going to see if she will come to dinner tonight at my mother's, and then I will propose."

"Derek, I think you might want to slow down a bit."

"Why? No, she is perfect."

"You just met her last night. Don't you think you should at least have another date?" Zac tries to calm Derek down.

"Wait—she is calling on the other line. I will call you back."

The phone rings again, and it's Derek. "What's up?" Zac answers.

Crying, Derek says, "I am not getting married to that woman. She just broke up with me."

"Wait, what? You got picked up at the bar. That does not make a relationship," Zac says.

"Whatever, Zac," he says and hangs up.

"What the fuck is going on with women these days?" Zac says out loud. Jake jumps off his chair and walks to the door, looks up at his leash, then turns to Zac. "Really? You went all over the bed last night. Now you want to go out?" Jake turns around, stares at Zac, lifts his leg, and pisses on his shoes. Jake returns to the chair and smirks at Zac. "I don't fucking believe it."

CHAPTER 12

Floor

*Z*ac awakes Friday morning with Jake sitting by the front door, staring at him. "OK, OK, I am coming." Zac throws on some dingy gray sweat pants and a matching hoodie, grabs the leash and Jake, and heads out to the street, on his way to the historic park catty-corner from the apartment.

Jake has been holding it for a while now and seeks the first opportunity to relieve himself. This opportunity comes at the corner near the park, not in the park. No, on the actual corner sidewalk, he curves his back, rear paws by his front paws. He looks up at Zac and lets it rip.

Now standing on a busy street corner, Zac reaches into his pocket for a baggie. "Shit." No baggie. It wouldn't matter—only a mop could clean this.

"What do you feed that thing?" a woman asks as she passes. Jake, feeling light and proud, begins jumping up at Zac, ready to go. Zac is stuck. He cannot leave it there but has nothing to clean it with.

"Gonna pick that up, aren't you?" asks a passing gentleman in a suit as he avoids the mess.

"Of course," Zac responds, not knowing what to do. He can't leave. There are too many people who have seen this. Zac bends his knees and leans down, looking at Jake. "You ready?"

Jake's ears perk, and he licks his lips and pauses like he is at the starting line of a hundred-meter race. Zac stands, removes his hoodie to reveal his shirtless chest, and drops the hoodie on the mess to cover it. "Go," he says, and they sprint toward the apartment.

Back in the apartment, Zac removes the leash and closes the door behind them. He knows this was wrong—after all, it cost him a hoodie. Jake jumps on the chair, looks out the window down to the corner of the park, then back at Zac with disappointment.

"What? You could have waited till the park."

Jake looks farther to his left behind him at the food on the counter and licks his lips.

"Really? Giving me shit about your shit, and now you want to stock up?" Zac retreats to the bathroom to shower and get ready for work.

Zac decides to add some color to his attire this day. He picks chocolate-brown soft cotton pants to start. He wears blue Gucci shaded leather lace ups over brown dress socks— sleek, stylish, and today's color with a classic shoe—not today's heavy-shoe novelty. A light-brown leather belt with a brass buckle finishes the lower half of his body. Zac reaches for a steel-blue pastel shirt and his tiny-checkered sand-and-hickory-colored tie to complete his attire. "I am not wearing a jacket today. It's Friday."

Exiting the bedroom, Zac notices Jake is no longer looking outside. He is now lying by his food dish. "OK, buddy," Zac says as he reaches for the food on the counter.

As Zac pours some food into Jake's dish, Jake rolls to his back with his belly exposed, looking for some TLC. Zac rubs his belly and picks him up, and they kiss each other good-bye. Zac exits and locks the door behind him.

Amanda enters his office while he's sitting with a cup of coffee and an energy bar. She hands him a travel drive and states, "These two books need reviewing. Can you get them done by Monday?"

"Sure, what are they?"

"Your favorite—love stories."

"Again? Come on, really?" he questions, wondering when this will stop.

"Yep, have fun," she says as she leaves his office. His phone rings. Answering it, he sees Adan is calling.

"Dude, we still on for tonight?" Adan asks.

"Yeah, about seven, right?" Zac confirms.

"Yeah. What are you doing?"

"Working, duh," Zac replies with a sour tone due to his most recent assignment.

"What are you reading this time?" Adan asks.

"Guess."

"No, dude, another tearjerker?" Adan teases.

"I don't know. I haven't read them yet."

"Them? You have more than one?" Adan questions, giggling.

"Whatever, dude. I got to go," Zac says, then hangs up.

Zac spends the morning reading the first book. It is another women's love story that he is not only tired of but kind of resents. He wonders why it is always the man's fault. Late morning has Zac feeling like he should stab himself in the eyes with a spork. Lunch is approaching, and Zac feels the weekend should start now. He turns off his computer, leaves the lights on, and departs from the intentionally inflicted sadness of the love stories he is growing to detest.

After a quick lunch, Zac walks to the Blue Soul. Knowing it is early and not really wanting to start drinking hard at this time, he thinks about having a drink and then heading home to relax before getting ready for tonight.

Entering the Blue Soul, Zac sees he is the only patron in the place. He takes a seat at the corner of the bar closest to the dance floor. Thomas is restocking the bar, cleaning, and generally setting the place up for a typical Friday night.

"What's up?" Thomas asks.

"Taking a little extra weekend," Zac responds.

"Starting now, are you?" Thomas replies as he dumps ice into the beer cooler.

"Yep," Zac breathes out.

"What can I get you?" Thomas asks.

"How about we start with a martini?"

"Sure, what you looking at?" Thomas asks.

"Vodka with an olive...and an onion."

Thomas reaches for the vodka and ices the glass. "You coming tonight?" he asks Zac.

"That's the plan," Zac says as he looks to the dance floor. Thomas completes the requested martini and places it in front of Zac. Zac takes a slow drink, sits back in his chair, and asks Thomas to turn on some music.

"All right, sure."

Zac relaxes as Thomas goes to the back to turn on the music system. The music starts to play, and Thomas returns, going about his business.

"What's up with that floor?" Zac asks.

"What about it?"

"The rose petals in the floor. Why are they there?"

Thomas freezes and looks over at Zac insecurely. He then walks down to the end of the bar where Zac sits. "Evil Woman" by the Electric Light Orchestra begins over the sound system. Thomas leans back against the backbar where the liquor bottles stand in front of a wall-length mirror. Taking a breath, he looks at Zac.

"You know my dad opened this bar in '55. My parents were married in '54. Dad used to bring a dozen roses to my mom every Friday. This lasted a couple of years. One Friday when Dad delivered roses to her, she started crying. Confused, my dad asked what was wrong. Was she OK? What was this about? She looked at him, crying, and said she appreciated the roses but they always died. She did not like the fact that the flowers were a sign of affection that then died. It bothered her. Dad kissed her on the forehead and walked off.

"The bar was open Saturdays but closed on Sundays back then. He decided to fix this. He had the staff come in on

Sunday, to their regret. He had twelve dozen roses when he arrived. They sanded the floor. Then he sat down and personally removed the petals from every one of the one hundred and forty-four stems. He spread them carefully around the floor. They then lacquered over the petals, keeping them in the floor. The sanding brought out a little lighter color in the wood floor that now contrasted with the red rose petals. After they were sealed to the floor, he closed the bar through the next Thursday and lacquered the floor every day until Wednesday. The floor looked encased in glass. On Thursday he waxed the floor so it could be danced on. Friday he asked Mom to come to the bar. Reluctantly, she did, expecting her weekly roses. When she arrived, he walked her to the dance floor and showed her what was done. He told her he was not bringing her roses anymore, but this floor was for her. She cried. This time they were happy tears."

"Wow," says Zac, completely stunned. He looks into his martini, takes a drink, and sits back. The door opens, and a woman in a graphite-colored dress, looking like her weekend is also about to start, walks in and sits in the middle of the bar.

Thomas looks to his left at her. "I'll be right with you," he says.

"Go ahead," Zac says, looking at the redhead to his right.

Thomas walks over and asks what he can get her. Zac, still taken aback, thinks, I read this shit every day.

Thomas makes the woman a drink and delivers it as the song ends. He walks back toward Zac.

"That's a hell of a story," Zac says.

"It's true," replies Thomas as he grabs the ice bucket and walks in the back. The bass opening of the Eagles' "I Can't Tell You Why" starts playing over the speakers. Thomas returns after a minute with fresh ice and pours it in the cooler.

"So what does Blue Soul mean?" asks Zac.

Thomas again leans on the rear bar, looking at Zac, and takes a hard, deep breath. The red-haired woman looks over at them.

"In '65," Thomas answers, "when I was two, my mother took me to her sister's home to play with my cousin. She was running errands, going to the bank to get change for the bar and make the deposit. You know, daily business. After the bank she was coming to the Soul. 'Soul' was the original name of this bar. On her way here a delivery truck lost its brakes and hit her side of the car. She died. Dad was devastated. He closed the bar for a week and sat alone on the dance floor, crying. After reopening the bar, he was never the same. He never dated another woman, and he just ran the bar daily. Not many smiles, just always serious and taking care of business. He made sure the bar was running with happy drunks, but he just remained emotionless, always the same. In '67, on the two-year anniversary of Mom's death, he changed the name to the Blue Soul. Nobody asked, and no comments were made."

Listening to the story, the red-haired woman's eyes begin to swell as she holds her tears.

Zac again stares at his martini and chooses to finish it with one drink. "I am sorry for you and your dad's loss, and I am sorry for asking," he says quietly.

"It's OK. It was a long time ago," Thomas says, looking to the woman at the bar.

"Did the truck driver die?" Zac asks, instantly realizing the insensitive nature of the question and his stupidity. Too late to take it back now.

Thomas quickly turns back to Zac. "No, he did not. He delivered beer to Dad three days a week for the next thirty years. Dad was not mad at him. He knew it was an accident, a mechanical failure. They got to know each other and had a beer together every day he delivered. They took time to sit. Sorry as the driver felt, Dad made sure every time he delivered there was time to sit. On Mom's birthday every year, they both relacquered the dance floor. Every year I do the same."

"That's rough. Again, maybe I should not have asked." Zac stands up, leaves some money on the bar, and turns to his right to walk out.

The redheaded woman is now struggling with her tears as she turns left toward Zac and delivers a look of anger and disappointment for his questions.

Zac walks by, and she turns to Thomas with eyes of compassion.

Thomas walks over to the woman. "It's OK. Don't worry about it. What's your name?" he asks with a mischievous smile.

Zac leaves the bar, turns left, and starts down the sidewalk. "That's what love is about, huh? Let's see what Jake has to say about that."

CHAPTER 13

Jake

*Z*ac unlocks his door and steps in, a little shocked Jake is not excited and waiting for him inside the door. "What's going on?" Zac calls. Jake appears to be asleep on his chair. "Jake, what's up?"

A lack of response sets fear in motion as Zac realizes there is a problem. Zac takes a couple of quick steps to Jake and then lightly shakes him to get his attention. Jake is unresponsive. Blood rushes through Zac. His heart races, and his perspiration, caused by his panic, increases exponentially. "Jake, Jake, you OK?" he asks, knowing he is not. Zac lifts Jake and rushes out the door.

He arrives at the veterinarian conflicted with emotions—tears, hope, and disbelief. The assistant immediately recognizes a problem and brings Jake and Zac to an examination room. She places Jake on a stainless steel table and begins her examination. As she listens for a heartbeat, she checks Jake's breathing and temperature. There are no signs of breathing, and Jake has no heartbeat.

Dr. Schreiber enters the room. She completes her round of tests and confirms Zac's fears. "He's gone. I am sorry."

Zac stands, reaches to the cold table, grabs Jake, and hugs him relentlessly. Jake's body heat contrasts with the table's coldness and provides hope as Zac realizes that whatever happened was recent, and surely there must be a solution. How could Jake, so full of life, rest in his arms, lifeless?

Questions fill Zac's mind. What happens now? Can anything be done to save Jake? What could he do to *fix* this? Skepticism and doubt creep into Zac. This cannot be. The lifeless Jake in his arms is not an entrance to tomorrow. Zac's palate swells, and tears stream his cheeks.

"I am so sorry. He is gone," Dr. Schreiber restates.

Zac's emotions take a quick turn as resentment and anger toward her appear. He does not want to accept it and certainly does not need to hear it again. He looks at her.

His clenching jaw, lowering eyebrows, and sharp eyes are enough, and she leaves the room. The assistant offers Zac all the time he needs and also leaves.

Now in the examination room alone, Zac feels isolated in a spotlight of life-changing moments. A U-turn of emotions enter him. "I love you, Jake," he says out loud. "You will always be the best. I am sorry I let you down. I love you so much. I don't know what to do. I miss you already." He just wants to cry out loud but won't allow himself. He lays Jake on the chair in the exam room. Jake will not be on a cold stainless table again. Zac understands he can't stay there. He needs some air, some space. He needs to breathe and is currently trapped by the situation in this heartless place. He wipes his tears and opens the door, calling to the assistant.

"What happens now?"

"Well, there is no charge for this," she states.

The emotional imbalance strikes again. He perceives this to be part of an insensitive, disassociated, and just cold place. "I am talking about Jake! I will pay for this. What about Jake?"

"We should discuss your wishes," she says.

Without hesitation he realizes the only way he can have part of Jake with him is through cremation. "I want him cremated," he blurts.

"I will be glad to take care of this. These run about seven hundred dollars. Is that OK?" she responds.

Now he can't get out of there soon enough. "Yes! When can I have him back?"

"About a week. I will call you."

The business end of this is over, to his relief. His anxiety is creating a reluctance to leave, knowing he has to leave Jake. This day never occurred to Zac. Jake was supposed to outlive him. At least, that was his expectation.

Zac leaves. Trying and failing to remain solid and stoic leads to crying. Climbing the stairs to his apartment, his question changes from why to what happened? Dialing the phone number as he climbs the stairs, anxiety returns as he approaches his door. Before he opens the door, the assistant at Dr. Schreiber's office answers the phone.

"What happened to Jake?" he asks.

"We will send him to a crematory as you wished."

"No, how did he die? What caused it?"

"I'm sorry. I mistook your question. We can perform an autopsy if you prefer."

"Yes, when?" He needs to know what caused this. She informs him it will be done next week, and she will call him upon completion. Standing outside his door, his eagerness to hear about the cause converts to fear and agitation. He will enter, knowing Jake is not there. A vacancy within him reflected by the apartment like a mirror.

The metal sound of the door latch amplifies to crystal clarity. All other sounds are drowned. The creaking of the door, which has gone unnoticed, now vibrates the door handle. Zac enters, refusing to look at the chair. The apartment is vacant. Nothing else matters.

Walking into the bedroom, Zac begins shedding his clothes. First his tie, then shirt. He kicks off his shoes, leaving them where they fall. Completing his change to a T-shirt and shorts, his dark socks remain, carelessly left on his feet. This means nothing at this moment.

Standing back in the living room, the longing desire for Jake creates deep, sad loneliness. It is a chance to breathe, albeit a shaky moment. Scanning the room, he sees to his right Jake's food on the counter, his food and water dishes on the floor, and Zac takes a look over his right shoulder to Jake's leather leash hanging to the left of those squeaking door hinges. Looking back toward his left, avoiding the chair, he sees on the counter the selfie Mary Ann took of the three of them. Remembering the moment reduces the hurt temporarily.

Zac retrieves a "whatever" beer from his refrigerator and grabs a beer glass. As he sits and turns on the television with the remote control, he decides the last thing he wants is external visual stimulation, so he changes it to a '70s rock channel. Pouring his beer with the requisite tipping of the glass, he listens as the guitar strings of a song increase in volume. Staring at the beer on the coffee table, Zac giggles slightly, remembering Jake's first and only drunk. The familiar acoustic guitar that begins Boston's "More Than a Feeling" is the culprit of further sadness. "It certainly is, Jake, more than a feeling," Zac says as he increases the volume.

The lyrics begin, and Zac attentively absorbs each line.

> *I woke up this morning and the sun was gone.*
> *Turned on some music to start my head*
> *I lost myself in a familiar song.*
> *I closed my eyes, and I slipped away.*

Zac realizes that this is just what happened. Jake is dead—his sun is gone. He is now lost in a familiar song, and he begins to slip away into acceptance of his lost Jake. Crying is now easy for him. No need to hold the tears, he cries with abandon.

> *It's more than a feeling*
> *More than a feeling*

> *When I hear that old song they used to play,*
> *More than a feeling*
> *Till I see Mary Ann walk away.*
> *I see my Mary Ann walkin' away.*

Zac now is trapped by the verse. He certainly has capitulated to the moment. This verse shakes his thoughts. He is living the moment as the past catches him.

> *So many people have come and gone.*
> *Their faces fade as the years go by.*
> *Yet I still recall as I wander on*
> *As clear as the sun in the summer sky.*

Zac's world is collapsed by the verses of a 1970s song that seem to point to his life.

> *It's more than a feeling*
> *More than a feeling*
> *When I hear that old song they used to play,*
> *More than a feeling*
> *Till I see Mary Ann walk away.*
> *I see my Mary Ann walkin' away.*

Crying uncontrollably, he looks up at the selfie. Seeing both Jake and Mary Ann at a time of sense makes him think to himself about how senseless he now feels.

When I'm tired and thinking cold
I hide in my music, forget the day
And dream of a girl I used to know.
I closed my eyes and she slipped away.

Lost in an emotional land he has never seen, he turns off the television and sits motionless in the now-dark apartment, in shock, pain, hurt, and anger. Day has fallen to night, and the helpless feelings inside cannot be cured with the beer. He lies on the couch and stares at the ceiling into the night.

Zac is awakened to his phone ringing. Lacking any sort of desire to see who it is, he turns it off and retreats to his bed. The day's events retrace within, sending tears to him once again. Eventually, he cries himself to sleep with the innocence of a child.

Morning arrives with the life of a new day and the absence of his best friend. Zac awakes with bloodshot, swollen eyes and a tear-saturated pillow. What next?

After lying in bed for minutes, which feel like hours, he forces himself to get out of bed. The careless wander into the living room is not the end but the beginning of a vacant place in time. Zac, completely disassociated with today, begins a necessary process. He grabs Jake's food off the counter and picks up his dishes off the floor—these reminders not only keep the sadness in him but anger him at the same time. He lifts the lid to the garbage, peers into the trash, and cannot believe he is about to throw them away. Full of regret, there is nothing to do, and he places the dishes first, then the food, in the container, gently so as not to insult or hurt Jake. Closing the lid to Jake's era, he turns and sees the leash hanging by the door. A frozen stare turns into a complete refusal to throw away the symbolic connection, the tie and the handle. The leash remains by the door.

Zac steps into the living room, shoulders fallen, a body hung on bones. Looking at the chair, the feeling of connection continues. He takes a seat in the chair and peers over his right shoulder. He realizes he is now in Jake's view, where Jake sat on the back of the chair and saw the outside world from within. Without Jake, he now gets to see the outside world from within, in many, many ways.

Hours slip by as Zac sits in Jake's chair in a semifetal position. Morning has gone, and early afternoon has Zac in the same shorts, sweat shirt, and dress socks, just gazing into the street. He watches everyone's Saturday from his curled, motionless position in Jake's chair. The gurgling in his stomach reminds him he is still alive, whether or not he wants to be. He gazes outside with sad, drooping eyes until he falls asleep.

Having slept awkwardly, Zac awakes with neck pain in the dark living room. Sitting upright in the chair, he stretches and tries to rotate his head left and right. The left is good. The right is stiff with pain and inflammation. This pain is meaningless. He sees no reason to acknowledge it, knowing it won't last as long as his emotional pain. He gets up, walks to the bedroom in the dark, and lands face first on the bed. Emotionally exhausted, he passes out on top of the bedspread.

The Sunday morning light appears through the bedroom window, glancing Zac's face. Reluctant acceptance sets in.

This recognition gives him limited energy—more than he had, but not a lot. He applies this to getting out of bed. "What's that smell?" he asks out loud as he sits on the edge of the bed. He stands, and the odor dissipates as he walks through the living room into the kitchen, thinking something must have rotted.

Opening the refrigerator, the smell returns. Nothing in the refrigerator is rotten. There is not enough food to spoil. Thinking there must be something in the garbage causing the odor, he lifts the lid—a hard reminder as he looks at Jake's food and dishes, but there is nothing in there rotting. Into the living room he walks. Surely it must be in there. The warm, flat beer still sits on the coffee table. Zac picks it up and carries it to the kitchen sink and pours it down. That must have been it.

He walks back to the living room, sits on the couch, and picks up his phone. Forgetting he had turned it off, he presses the power button and awaits its response. While he waits, the odor returns. He smells his shirt, under his arms, and his shorts—and there it is. Fuck, really? It is him. He paces to the shower and removes the socks, shirt, and shorts. He reaches in, turns on the water, and steps in.

Drying himself after his shower, he ponders. What will today bring? He can't sit here all day. The gym. That's it. Putting on some jeans, a T-shirt, gym socks, and loafers, he grabs his gym bag and moves toward the living room. Checking his phone, he sees two messages. Oh well, only two means they can't be important. He ignores them. Into the kitchen he treads, seeking a protein shaker from the cabinet. Adding two scoops of chocolate protein and half a glass of warm water, he screws on the lid and shakes. Slamming the protein shake, he throws the shaker into the sink, grabs his wallet and keys, and leaves.

After changing to his gym clothes in the locker room and walking into the gym, Zac looks around, deciding what to do. Squeezing his earphones in, he reaches for his phone, turns on Pandora, and seeks a genre. Avoiding the '70s rock theme that previously struck him, he hits '80s rock, hoping to jack himself up for the ensuing workout. Deciding to warm up with light bench-pressing, he loads twenty-five pounds on each side of the barbell and lies on the bench, the barbell above him.

Def Leppard's "Animal" begins to play. "Thank God," he says out loud, thinking he could use a song like this right now. A song about lust is exactly the key. Strong now, a man's song brings him out of his solemnness. Lifting the barbell off the pegs, he brings it to his chest and pushes up. He feels better, avoiding the whirlwind thoughts, conversations, and emotions of the last two days. He racks the weight, gets off the bench, adds to the weight, and proceeds. Another set. Yes, this is what he needs. Again, he adds more weight, slides onto the bench, and starts. "Animal" ends, although he is not done.

Next plays the Scorpions' "Still Loving You."

"Great," Zac says with disdain. A love song. In the middle of a set, he cannot change to another song. The familiar guitar riff begins, and he just continues to press the weights. As the lyrics start, he racks the bar and listens.

Time, it needs time
To win back your love again.
I will be there; I will be there.
Love, only love
Can bring back your love someday.
I will be there; I will be there.

I'll fight, babe; I'll fight
To win back your love again.
I will be there; I will be there.
Love, only love
Can break down the wall someday.
I will be there; I will be there.

If we'd go again
All the way from the start
I would try to change
The things that killed our love.
Your pride has built a wall, so strong
That I can't get through.
Is there really no chance
To start once again?
I'm loving you.

Try, baby, try
To trust in my love again.
I will be there; I will be there.
Love, our love

Just shouldn't be thrown away.
I will be there; I will be there.

If we'd go again
All the way from the start
I would try to change
The things that killed our love.
Your pride has built a wall, so strong
That I can't get through
Is there really no chance
To start once again

If we'd go again
All the way from the start
I would try to change
The things that killed our love
Yes, I've hurt your pride, and I know
What you've been through.
You should give me a chance.
This can't be the end.
I'm still loving you.
I'm still loving you; I need your love.
I'm still loving you.

Stunned, Zac does not know what to think. His reddened eyes begin to swell with tears. One more set, he thinks. Clear this up. The weights are so heavy now. Did someone add some weight?

He is still loving Jake, thinking about Jake, and thinking this is about Jake. Is it, or is this a gift from Jake? Some weight was added, just not at the gym. He turns off the music, clears the weights, and walks to the locker room. Sitting on the bench in thought, he does not change his clothes. He clutches his bag, puts his street clothes in it, grabs his keys, and walks out. Leaving the gym, out of the blue he blurts, "Is that what Jake says about it?"

CHAPTER 14

Confuse

*A*rriving back at home, Zac's empty feelings push him in. He turns on the television to some mindless news channel. The world news certainly does not affect his painful world. Reaching for his phone, he decides to check the messages. The first, from Friday night, is Adan questioning where he is. Erasing the first message, he proceeds to the next. Adan again. "Dude, what happened to you last night? Call me." What does it matter? Missing a Friday night out is meaningless compared to who he misses now. He calls Adan just to get it over with.

"Dude, where have you been?" Adan asks.

Zac pauses for a couple seconds. "Home."

"What's going on?" Adan asks.

"Jake died," Zac states quietly and quickly.

"What? Oh, Zac, that's fucked up. I'm sorry. When?"

"Friday," Zac says as his heart softens. "You know, I really don't want to talk about this now. We'll hook up this week."

"All right, dude—call me if you need anything."

"Thanks. See you." Zac returns to Jake's chair for a few minutes with the uncomfortable feeling he has to do something, so he gets up and lies on the couch and does nothing. The day produces a Zac that goes from the living room to the bedroom repeatedly, accomplishing nothing and cementing his depression.

Monday morning Zac can't wait to get out of the apartment. He shows up at work an hour early and realizes he still has to review the other love story he had passed on for an early Friday. He starts the coffee and returns to his office. Cranking up his computer, he thinks he might be able to get through this before Amanda arrives. "Come on. I can suck this up," he says, trying to encourage himself. He opens the file and begins reading.

Two hours later Zac is midway through the book. This novel is different. It seems to slowly suck him in like quicksand. While he is engrossed, or at least he thinks he is, Amanda rears her lovely self.

Walking into his office, she asks, "You get them done?"

"First one sucks. Halfway through the second," he says as he avoids looking directly at her.

She notices Zac is projecting a different energy, and she sits down. Zac now has to look at her. Shit, he thinks, she never does this.

"Is this one getting to you?" she pries.

He returns to reading.

"Looks like it to me."

"I will let you know in an hour. You OK with that?" Zac questions with an attitude that should tell her to fuck off.

"Yeah," she replies, slightly confused but intrigued, and she decides to remain seated. Ten minutes of hard silence pass. She tries to assess what is going on with him. Is this book that she previously reviewed and found mediocre at best really getting to him?

Feeling the walls enclosing, he stands up quickly. "Done. It sucks like all the rest," he says, hoping this will get her out of his office.

Startled, she now knows something is wrong. "You OK?" she asks with a noticeable reduction in her titanium.

He sits down. "Yeah, I will be all right."

"You will be?" she asks as she notices a sort of resignation in his countenance. She remains seated.

Zac thinks, why can't she just leave? He silently stares at her.

"What's going on?" She has never seen him like this.

He does not want to exhibit any kind of weakness, yet it is overpowering him. He fights it internally as he stares at her. She remains seated and silent. Zac sits and puts his elbows on the desk and his head in his hands, looking down at the desk. "Jake died."

"Go home," she orders as she rises from the chair.

He thinks that is the last place he wants to be.

"Take a couple of days. I am sorry for your loss." She turns and begins to walk out of his office. "Really, I am sorry."

She leaves the office and walks down the hall as her eyes redden, remembering her shoes.

Zac does not know what to do as he leaves the building. Finally able to breathe after suffering through Amanda, he decides to hit the gym and get the blood flowing. At the gym he realizes his gym bag is at home. "Shit," he says aloud. "Fuck it. I will work out in my work clothes."

Heading into the gym, he presses in his headphones. He does not turn on any music. He doesn't need more meaningful music. He just doesn't want anyone to talk to him. A leg workout, he thinks. No, not in his suit pants. He rolls up his sleeves and begins an arm workout instead. The earphones do not silence his surroundings. He can hear people close to him.

"What the hell is he doing?" he hears a guy say. Blowing it off, he continues. Mumbling surrounds him. What does he care? He is not there for their entertainment.

"Wow, he's working out in style," a woman says to her friend in a sarcastic tone. He doesn't care and pushes through. His workout finished with a sweaty and stained shirt, he simply leaves feeling he finally completed something positive.

Zac arrives home with time not filled—a vacant apartment, an afternoon of space, alone. Saddened, he starts cleaning the apartment. Get it done, he thinks. At least this is something productive. He decides he is going to work tomorrow, thinking this will sedate his heart.

The rest of the week is a bad rerun. Wake up, work, home. It helps him slow down the constant thoughts about Jake and how sudden and unexpected his death was. Friday morning, while in his office, he calls Adan.

"You OK?" Adan answers.

"Yeah, just at it, you know. You got time for lunch?" he asks.

"Sure, dude, what time?" Adan replies lightly.

"Let's do twelve thirty," Zac says, kind of hoping this might be an opportunity to make the lunch linger and screw off the rest of the day.

"All right, see you then."

Adan arrives earlier than Zac. Sitting in the restaurant waiting for Zac, he begins to wonder if Zac is really OK. A look of concern crosses his face as Zac sits down.

"What's up?" Zac asks, sitting in the booth across from Adan.

"Same old, you know," Adan responds, leafing through the menu.

Zac investigates the menu, avoiding the Jake tension between them.

After ordering Adan asks, "You all right? I know this is tough."

"Yeah, it's been a rough week. I'll be OK. What's been going on with you?"

"Just work. Haven't been out since last Friday. Haven't really felt like it." Adan dances around the conversation. "Thomas told us to thank you. Something about a redhead you left him with last Friday. Talked about how he comforted her after you left."

"What a fucker. Every time you turn around, he is hitting something else. Playing her emotions. You think he is happy or sad, sport fucking twenty-five-year-olds?"

"Really, of course he's good. We could be so lucky at his age."

"Yeah, I guess," Zac replies as it hits him. He does not want to be out sport fucking. He begins contemplating this. He was happy with Mary Ann, although she was not available to him for a still unknown reason. Picking up girls stroked his ego and confidence but weakened him emotionally. He really starts to think about what he has done.

Adan interrupts his thoughts. "I haven't had time to tell you. Guess what? Mary Ann broke up with her boyfriend."

"So, what do I care?" Zac states abruptly, but he's thinking this could be good, perhaps an opportunity, a door to open.

"You really don't care?"

"Whatever, dude. How do you know?" Zac asks.

Adan is a little careful—he found out the same day Jake died. "Friday we were at the Blue Soul having a few, when Mary Ann and the girls showed up. She looked a little bothered and relieved at the same time. They all came up to the bar and ordered shots of tequila. You know shit's up when they start. They were right by me, avoiding Derek, which was funny. Anyway, I asked how she was and what's going on. She said she broke up with her boyfriend and it felt good. She popped another shot, and they all took seats at the bar. You know that's not like them. Sitting at the bar? She did not elaborate, and you could tell she was not going to."

Zac's phone rings, interrupting the conversation.

"Hello, this is Zac."

"Zac, this is Dr. Schreiber."

Zac freezes, without words.

"Zac, are you there?"

"Yes, I am," he says in a shaky voice.

"Zac, I wanted to give you the results of Jake's autopsy."

Zac saddens deeply. Jake is dead, and he has been working to both accept it and pretend it is not true simultaneously.

"OK, go ahead," he softly speaks.

"Jake passed from an aneurysm. It was apparently pretty quick."

Zac's eyes redden. He is stunned, even a little relieved, knowing this is nothing he could have prevented. "What kind? Never mind." His voice changes with his palate swelling. "When can I pick him up?"

"Probably Monday. We have sent him to the crematory already and should have him soon. We will call you when he is back."

He hangs up without words, looks to Adan, throws twenty bucks on the table, and says, "I am not hungry. Sorry." He walks out.

Adan just sits, thinking about how this could possibly be hitting Zac harder than either of them think.

CHAPTER 15

Keep

*M*onday morning at work, Zac's phone rings. "This is Zac."

"Zac, this is Dr. Schreiber's office. We have Jake's remains here."

Zac, not wanting to become overwhelmed, replies immediately. "I will pick him up this afternoon."

At lunchtime he walks to Amanda's office. "I have to pick up Jake. I won't be back until tomorrow."

"That's fine, Zac. Again, I am really sorry. He was special."

"He still is," Zac replies as he turns to leave.

He walks into the veterinarian's office and sees the assistant at the desk. She looks up. "Let me get him for you," she says and disappears into a back office. She brings out a tin box with roses painted on it and a card tied to it with "Jake" on it. Zac's eyes begin to tear up as she hands it to him. She says, "He had a ventricular aneurysm—basically, his heart broke." He takes the tin with both hands, not wanting to drop his best friend, and says nothing.

On the way home he decides he wants Jake in something special, not some fucking tin box. Walking down his street, three blocks from his apartment, he sees an antique store named Heirloom. He has seen the store before but had thought nothing of it. He walks in carrying Jake, seeking something special for him.

Wandering through the store, he views many items. Nothing seems to feel suitable. He asks the salesclerk if she has any urns.

"No, we don't. I'm sorry."

As he turns to walk out, he sees what looks like an egg sitting in a stand. He approaches, trying to obtain a better look. As he reaches it, he sees it is a pewter egg with elaborate vines wrapped around it. It's held up by a stand that looks like the stem entering the roots of the vine. The top of the egg has an attached lid that opens just the top quarter of it. One vine leaf sits curling over as the handle to the lid.

"How much is this?" he asks, turning to the woman.

"That is really old. That was made in the eighteen hundreds in France," she states.

"That's not what I asked."

"Well, that is really expensive. That has been here for—"

He cuts her off. "How much is it?" He really needs to know, although it probably won't matter.

"We have been asking a thousand dollars for that, but I will sell it for eight hundred, if it helps."

"Done," he says as he reaches for his credit card.

Walking back home, he sees the little Honda with the "I love my Border Terrier" sticker in the middle of the rear window. Feelings and memories begin to consume his mind and heart. Remembering how Jake acted by the car and the look he gave Zac pulls at him. Zac starts crying as he walks past the car.

Zac arrives at home, crying desperately. His best friend is now gone, and his emptiness is swallowing him. He takes the tin with blurry, teary eyes and opens it as he sits in Jake's chair. He sees Jake's remains in a plastic bag. He can't control his tears as they stream from his eyes, and his nose starts running. He grabs the egg and opens the top. Looking into it, he takes the bag, opens it, and pours Jake into the egg. He closes it and places it next to the selfie behind the chair, then leans the selfie on it.

Zac sits in Jake's chair, remembering his buddy. He did not have Jake for many years, but the time he did have with him was really meaningful. As he sits in Jake's chair staring into the universe, he decides to turn on some music. "More Than a Feeling" comes on again like it's a message. This time he has Jake with him. He starts to think about the mischief Jake achieved and laughs in between tears. The shoes, the dress, the office, and even the shitting on the bed run through his mind. Throughout the song he thinks about how good a friend Jake was. He didn't know it when Jake was alive, but he now knows how much he loved Jake and, more importantly, how much Jake loved him. As the song ends, he starts crying uncontrollably and stands up. Turning to look at Jake, he says, "I miss you, my boy. I love you so much. I will always keep you."

CHAPTER 16

Breaks

*O*ut for lunch, Adan walks by a sandwich shop and spies Allison inside. Alone, he decides to retrace his steps and offer lunch. "Care to join me for lunch?" he asks. "It's on me."

"OK, sure."

After choosing their lunch, they sit together. "Thank you for lunch. How have you been?" she asks.

"All right. Just keeping busy with work. How about you?"

"Keeping track of all those employees, are you?" she teases.

"Yeah, that's it," he replies, smiling.

"You know Mary Ann broke up with Enrique, right?" she asks.

"Yeah, she told me at the Blue Soul when you girls had a mission at the bar."

"So did you tell Zac?"

"Yes, I did. He has had a rough time since Jake died. He wasn't very responsive," he says solemnly.

"Jake died? Really? Does Mary Ann know?" she replies nervously.

"I don't know. I don't know if he called her. He's pretty devastated."

"She has not said anything to me about it. She has been a little emotional since the breakup though."

"I figured it would be best if he told her."

"I don't know. I think she would want to know. She really loved him. Do you think I should let her know?" she asks intently.

"I don't know."

A few moments of silence take place, with both realizing this has an impact.

"I am going to her place tonight for some girl time. I don't know if I can withhold this. This sucks. I don't think she will be able to handle this."

"If you tell her, you know she is going to be pissed at Zac. I really think this is up to him."

"OK, you are right." She sighs deeply.

Allison arrives at Mary Ann's apartment to comfort her friend after the breakup. "I have Ben and Jerry's in five flavors," she says as she steps into the kitchen.

"Yippee," Mary Ann says in jest.

"What flavor do you want?" Allison asks Mary Ann.

"Ah, I only get one?"

"No! We can mix them up if you want or go one after the other. Whatever you say."

Mary Ann takes out a couple of spoons from the drawer and hands one to Allison. "What are you waiting for?" she asks Allison.

"I'm getting there. Those stupid plastic wraps around the top. Why do they do that? Don't they know when women need this, we really need this?" Allison answers.

They sit down and pass the ice-cream buckets back and forth to each other, trying the flavors.

"How are you doing?" Allison asks Mary Ann, being her best friend for the breakup.

"Better now. Enrique was just a jerk. He was always late, always wanted either me to pay or we had to split the bill. I just bought a new car. I can't afford to be taking his ass out. What a man," she replies with ice cream in her mouth.

"He was nice to us. I don't get it. He always seemed really nice."

"Yeah, well, I think it was his game. You know, he was nice to all of you and disconnected to me. Some kind of pressure, I think. All my friends like him, so I am expected to stay with him," she explains.

"Well, as long as you are good being away from him, that's all that counts. Can I have his phone number?" Allison jokes, laughing.

"Bitch," Mary Ann says, laughing along. "Why do we do this?"

"Do what?"

"Attack Ben and Jerry like we are pissed at them for the breakup. All it does is make us work out harder later to get rid of the added ass. It's messed up. I am not doing this anymore. I have a better idea." Mary Ann reaches into a cabinet above the kitchen sink and retrieves an unopened bottle of Jameson whiskey.

"Well, it's your night. If you think it's best," Allison concedes.

"I don't know if it's best, but I think it is better," she says as she opens the bottle.

"I will put this away," Allison says with caution, referring to the ice cream.

They decide there is no need for shot glasses and begin to drink straight from the bottle. After a couple of gulps, Allison remembers her earlier conversation with Adan. She becomes concerned and wants to tell Mary Ann about Jake. She reluctantly elects not to. She does not want Mary Ann going through the breakup with Enrique and then dealing with Jake's death while they drink heavily.

"Do you want to watch a movie?" Allison asks, thinking this is what women do after breakups.

"No, sitting around crying over some love story doesn't sound like fun. I am going to put on some music." Mary Ann goes to her computer with plugged-in speakers. "What do you want to hear?" she asks.

"Taylor Swift."

"God, no. No way. I am not going to listen to her relationship problems masked by some song. Hell no." She puts on Journey.

"This is better?" Allison questions.

"Oh yeah. After this, maybe we will put on some Michael Jackson, Bon Jovi, Foreigner, maybe even the Babys. I don't know. We'll have to see how it goes." She giggles.

After an hour of drinking straight from the bottle like any non-self-respecting woman would do, the night becomes a blur. They have been chatting it up, talking about men and why they are so difficult. Drunk enough to start slurring her words, Allison decides she now needs some ice cream. She grabs the closest bucket out of the freezer, picks up her previous spoon, and goes for it.

"None for me. I don't want to have to run an extra mile due to this," Mary Ann slurs, wobbling.

"This is so good," Allison chimes as she starts to slip. She puts down the ice cream and stumbles toward Mary Ann. Tripping on a rug, she falls toward her. Mary Ann helps her remain upright. Hugging each other, Allison looks at Mary Ann and kisses her.

Mary Ann, stunned, doesn't stop her, but she really is not into women.

Allison's throat begins to sour, and she throws up a little bit of vomit into Mary Ann's mouth.

"What the fuck?" Mary Ann asks, spitting as she pushes her away, and Allison falls to the floor. While Allison begins recognizably heaving, Mary Ann grabs her under her arms and assists her to the bathroom. Allison vomits heavily into the toilet with a ripe smell of Irish whiskey and chocolate-chunk ice cream. Mary Ann holds her hair back, sitting adjacent to her.

"I don't believe this. I am holding a woman's hair at the toilet. I thought this was the man's job," Mary Ann says with wobbly words.

Waking in the morning next to each other in bed, their heads are spinning with epic hangovers, and they are quite probably still drunk. Allison looks at Mary Ann to her right, wondering what happened. "Did we do anything last night?" she asks.

"Like what?" Mary Ann responds without movement of any kind.

"Did we have sex last night?" asks Allison, completely distraught and afraid of the answer.

"No, we didn't."

"Oh, OK,"

After a few moments of silence, while they suffer with putting last night back together, Allison grows insecure.

"Aren't I hot enough?" she asks Mary Ann.

Mary Ann remains silent for a few minutes. "You kissed me last night. When you did, you threw up a little in my mouth. Fucking gross. Then I had to hold your hair in the bathroom and smell your vomit. Nobody is that hot."

Uncomfortable silence captures the room as they lie next to each other.

"I better go." Embarrassed, Allison gets out of bed and reaches for her clothes.

Mary Ann looks at her and then rolls over, thinking she should sleep this off. "Lock it when you leave," she says as Allison stumbles toward the front door.

CHAPTER 17

Surprise

*A*llison and Mary Ann's girls' night came with positive consequences, not just hangovers. Mary Ann's jump into the Enrique relationship clouded the closure of her relationship with Zac. She internally compares the two and realizes she was not fair to Zac. Not only did she jump into another relationship immediately after Zac, they never had the opportunity to discuss what happened.

As her empathy for Zac grows, she feels sour about herself. She questions why she jumped into another relationship so quickly. Then she really questions herself about why she broke up with Zac anyway. He was great, he treated her great, they had a great connection, and she broke it off. Over what—a bad dance? Allison's comments? Her internal struggle with feminism? Enrique was a jerk and easy to get over. This breakup has her thinking about Zac, not Enrique.

The following Thursday, Mary Ann has reconciliation on her mind. Not with Zac—she has given that up, which is the only way forward—but with Allison. And internally she has to get past why she broke up with Zac. If nothing else, so she will not make this mistake again. She calls Allison.

"Hi there, how are you?" she asks Allison. They haven't spoken since the awkward night of vomit tasting.

"Good. I have been meaning to call you. I feel so bad about the night at your place. I am so sorry. I got a little hammered, and the ice cream——"

Mary Ann cuts her off. "Don't worry about it. It's fine. That's not why I am calling. Can we meet for a drink after work?"

"Sure. How about five thirty?"

"Great, let's go to the Blue Soul. I will see you there."

Mary Ann feels bad about the Zac breakup, but the recognition is allowing her to get a foundation under her feet again. She has to move forward. She doubts she'll reconnect with Zac; however, she does miss Jake and would like to see him again. She thinks maybe she should contact Zac and offer to take Jake for a walk or perhaps even for the weekend. First things first—she needs to talk with Allison. Not for the blame game that everyone is so interested in these days, just so she can understand herself and be better at any possible relationship. She wants to clear the air so Allison will understand that though she made a mistake, Mary Ann is willing to move past it. The air around her lightens.

Entering the Blue Soul, Mary Ann greets Thomas as she passes the bar. In doing so she also mouths the word "Corona" so he will know her order before she sits. She makes her way to Allison, sitting in the front corner by the dance floor. "Hi, hottie," she tells Allison in reassurance after her night over as she sits.

"Hi, what's going on?" Allison asks.

"We'll get to that in a minute. Did you get a drink? I ordered a beer when I passed the bar. Do you need anything?" Mary Ann looks around for a waitress.

"Yeah, I ordered a beer too. Don't want to get drunk tonight."

Thomas brings the ordered drinks over and offers to pour them. "No, thanks," Mary Ann states as she takes a drink from the bottle. Allison agrees, and the glasses are removed.

"Why are you bringing these?" Allison asks Thomas, referring to the vacancy of a waitress.

"She got into an accident on the way here tonight. She's OK, nothing major. But I figured it's Thursday night, and I don't expect a lot tonight, so I told her to take the night off and that I will still pay her what she normally makes."

Allison and Mary Ann both smile. "You really are a nice guy," Mary Ann states.

"Yeah, I guess. Just don't reveal it, please?"

"OK. Your secret is safe with us," Allison says, smirking.

"Anyway, I need her here on Saturday, so she needs to recuperate. Oh, I haven't had time to tell you. Saturday night I have something special lined up. You girls will love it, so I hope you can make it," he says, full of excitement.

"OK, I can. How about you?" Mary Ann asks Allison.

"Sure."

"Thanks, girls. These two are on me." He retreats to the bar.

"You look good. What's going on?" Allison asks.

"I just came to some conclusions, and I wanted to run them by you."

"OK. You are a little bubbly, so I am sure it's good. Come on. Give it up."

"Well, you know, after I broke up with Enrique, I had some time to think about things. You know the postbreakup disgust. Why was I with him? What did I see in him? Why did I even stay that long? You know all that insecure bullshit," Mary Ann says.

"Yeah, so?"

"Well, why did I break up with Zac?"

Silence enters the conversation.

"I am sorry," Allison says. "I really did—"

Mary Ann cuts her off. "It was not you. I didn't break up with Zac because of you. Sorry, you're not that hot," she teases. "I am not even sure why I broke up with him. Maybe I wasn't ready. I don't know. What I do know now is that not being my own woman does not make me 'that woman.' And being my own woman means I can also have a man. These are not exclusive, and they should not be. I have been thinking about this. I want a man. My desires don't make me less of a woman. Nor does being a woman make me less of a person, and neither of these make a man superior, in my mind."

"Is this the root of man hating? We neglect our desires because we think they make men feel superior, or women inferior. Then we are pissed because of it and blame men."

Mary Ann notices Allison's contemplative eyebrows and continues. "So I have decided that I won't sacrifice myself for a cause. I will have a man if I want, or, for that matter, a woman." She winks at Allison, joking. "I do refuse to be pissed at men just for being men. If they are sexist, that's another issue. Aren't we being sexist due to the progression of feminism and what it has evolved to? That's not right either. So please forgive my lack of future participation." Mary Ann reaches for her beer and takes a breath in relief.

"OK, I am sorry. I didn't think you should have broken up with Zac, and I feel it was my fault," Allison says with regret.

"It wasn't. It was mine. Wow, I feel better now." Mary Ann takes a swig of her beer. "So, Saturday night something big is happening, huh? Wonder what's going on?"

Perplexed about numerous things, Allison says, "Guess we will find out."

"I got to go. I have papers to grade. See you Saturday?"

"Of course," Allison spouts as she finishes her beer.

Adan and Zac enter the Blue Soul and go straight to the bar moments after Mary Ann and Allison depart.

"You guys just missed Allison and Mary Ann," Thomas relays.

"Good," Adan replies.

Zac thinks about how awkward this could have been. "Why are we here? What did Derek want?" he asks Adan.

"I don't know. He asked what we were doing tonight and if we could meet him here."

"You guys need a drink?" Thomas asks.

"Yeah, sure. How about a couple of Coronas?" Zac says.

"Huh," Thomas mumbles to himself as he reaches into the cooler.

"I want to be in early tonight," Zac says to both men as Thomas plops the beer bottles onto the bar. "When is he supposed to be here?"

"Anytime now. I'll call him." He reaches for his phone and dials Derek's number.

"Good evening," Derek answers ever so properly.

"When are you going to be here?" Adan questions.

"We will be there soon," he replies.

"We?" Adan asks.

"My mother is joining us."

"OK, dude. Whatever." Adan hangs up. "They're on their way," he says. "His mother is coming too."

"All right, let's get a table then," Zac quips.

"Hey, guys, I have something cool happening Saturday night. Can you guys make it? You are not going to want to miss this," Thomas says.

"Yeah, what's up?" Adan asks.

"A friend is in town. Trust me—this will be cool."

"All right, we will be here. Let's get a table," says Zac.

They depart the bar and acquire the table closest to the bar. The two sit, looking around. It's a dead night, with them and Thomas making three people in the whole bar.

The door opens, and Derek and his mother, Dora, arrive. Zac and Adan stand and greet Dora and acknowledge Derek. They sit down and await Thomas for a cocktail order. Dora is glowing and obviously happy. Zac thinks maybe Derek has found his woman and this is Dora's announcement to make.

"What can I get you two?" Thomas asks.

"I will have a tequila sunrise, and my mother will have a Tom Collins," Derek replies happily.

Thomas shakes his head as he walks toward the bar. Dora retires to the ladies' room to freshen up as the cocktails are made. She returns to her seat just as Thomas delivers the drinks.

"What are those glasses you are wearing? We are in a bar. I don't think you need sunglasses," Adan says to Derek.

"These are vintage rose-colored glasses. Aren't they cool?" Derek replies.

"Oh shit," Zac interjects. "So what's up?" Zac would rather be at home.

"You guys remember my sister, Stephanie, and her friend Julie, don't you?" Derek asks.

Zac and Adan nod their heads without words as fear creeps in.

"Well, we have good news," Derek continues. "Stephanie is pregnant. We are so happy, and we wanted to personally thank you, Adan," he says as Dora smiles happily.

Adan hangs his head, then looks up at Zac and Derek, avoiding eye contact with Dora. "What the fuck?" Adan states with reserved anger due to Dora's presence. "You knew about that night. Did you set us up, you fucker?" Adan is now shaking in anger.

"Um, no," Derek answers shakily, worried about Adan's state of mind and how this news will affect their friendship— and how it just might affect his physical wellness.

"Wait!" says a startled Zac, thinking about his own predicament. "What about Julie?" he asks.

Derek responds, looking at Zac, "Julie is not pregnant. You might want to get checked."

CHAPTER 18

Finally

*F*riday morning arrives with relief and grief—Zac feeling relief and Adan grief. Both are wobbly about the revelation.

Zac, sitting in his office, is afraid to call Adan; however, he realizes he has no choice. Zac lifts his phone and dials.

Adan answers with a solemn hello.

"Adan, how are you doing?" Zac asks.

"As good as I can. I don't know what to do. I guess I am in shock."

"Yeah, that was shocking. What the fuck was up with Derek and his mother? I don't even know what to say. They assume this is happy news. It might be for them, but—Julie told me she was on birth control. Stephanie told you the same, right?"

"Yes. I asked her twice. This is not cool. Now what am I going to put in my ledger?" Adan asks with all seriousness.

"What? Really, that is your concern? So a child is not crossing your mind?" Zac asks, surprised.

"What am I to do? I don't even have Stephanie's number, and she is married to Julie. You really think she wants me involved? You and I both know this was a setup. So what am I supposed to do? Chase her down, have a talk with her, and pretend she had some sort of interest? If she did, she would have been there last night, or she could have got my number from Derek and called me. I mean, really, I should see Derek and get to the bottom of this. Then I can beat his pretty face unrecognizable."

"Come on, Adan. You don't want to have that hanging on you after this."

"Yeah, Zac, you are right. I think I should just buy a couple cases of condoms," Adan replies, defeated.

"I will call Derek to get to the bottom of this. This smells bad, and I really don't need Derek around for a while. So if he gets pissed, I really don't care."

"All right, Zac. I will talk to you later."

Zac is pissed and thinks about how this life-changing event could have been his. He sits back in his chair as Amanda walks in.

"Good morning. How are you this fine Friday?" she asks.

Thinking he may be assigned some seriously bad stories, he decides to remain calm and friendly. "Good. How are you? Do you have any plans this weekend?" he asks, enthused.

"Not really. I was thinking about going to the Blue Soul you guys hang out at. I heard something special is going to happen Saturday. Do you know anything?" she asks, entertained.

"I heard the same. Adan and I are going to check it out, so maybe it would be fun if you showed your charming self," Zac says reluctantly.

"We'll see. Anyway, I wanted to let you know that I am taking you off love patrol. You aren't any good at it anyway. So I am giving you back the thrillers and whatever you like."

"Don't fuck with me, Amanda. Really?" Zac finally can breathe, if she is serious.

"Yeah, you've been through enough. Have fun this weekend. You know, I won't have time to assign you anything for the rest of the day. So clear what you are working on and send it to me. You have been through a lot the past few months, and I am not sure I helped. So if you are OK with it, take the day off and do something. Maybe I will see you Saturday."

"Um, OK. Thanks," he says as Amanda leaves the office. "She does have a heart. I never knew," he says out loud to himself.

He decides he should call Derek before he leaves. He lifts his phone, takes a deep breath, and dials.

"Good morning," Derek answers.

"Derek, you need to come clean with me. That was fucked up, and I am not at all sure what the fuck happened."

"All right. I first need to tell you I had no idea. The night we went out, I thought we were all doing just that. I did not know about you and Adan going home with Julie and Steph. You know they are married, don't you?"

"Yeah, I found out," Zac answers.

"They said nothing about it for weeks. I really thought you all had fun dancing and the night ended."

"So you did not set this up?"

"No, I did not."

"Then what happened?"

"Stephanie came over to the house last week and informed Mother and me that she was pregnant. We were both shocked. After quite a difficult conversation, she told us the only man she had been with was Adan, and Julie was with you that night. Now I am not saying this was right or defending them, but we have another member of the family to welcome, and my mother is now so happy. So maybe we got ahead of ourselves and informed you in a most inappropriate way. Maybe Stephanie should have done it, but she does not want Adan around. She does not want anything from him, and you know we are financially fortunate, so that is not an issue."

"I don't even know what to say. So it's all Stephanie's and Julie's choice. Financially and physically, Stephanie and Julie are good? What about Adan? What if he wants to be involved? What then?" Zac asks angrily.

"I don't know. Maybe I should call Adan."

"No, don't. I don't think he would be OK with it now."

"Well, maybe I can talk with him Saturday night," Derek says.

"I don't think you should show up Saturday. Maybe you and Stephanie should discuss it and have Stephanie call Adan. Otherwise, I think you should give Adan some time."

"OK. How is Adan?" Derek asks.

"Pretty shaken. I don't even know if he wants to be involved, but Stephanie should offer the discussion at least. Who knows—maybe everyone involved is OK with this. I don't know. A little time to clear some heads could be productive."

"OK, Zac. You are right. I will talk to Stephanie and figure some things out. Have a good weekend."

Zac hangs up without acknowledgment.

He still has the responsibility of calling Adan and disclosing his conversation with Derek. So he decides to clear this air before he leaves, and he calls Adan. "Adan, I just spoke with Derek."

"And?"

"Well, I don't know. I think Derek was as shocked as we were. This was not a setup by Derek—maybe Stephanie and Julie, but not Derek and his mom. He said they want nothing from you, financially or otherwise. He is going to talk to Stephanie, and maybe she will call you."

"So you mean I might actually still get to use my ledger?" Adan asks, excited.

"What the fuck? You know what? I will see you tomorrow." Zac hangs up, relieved and in disbelief.

Zac thinks he has dodged a bullet while he works out. At home, cleaning, he sees Jake's urn and the selfie and realizes he was blessed to have had Jake in his life. The sadness and depression are dissipating, even though he misses Jake terribly. He decides Amanda was right. He has been through a lot, and now he wants to move forward—not forget, just accept.

The night is approaching, and he decides to watch a movie and chill in. He turns on the television, and showing on a movie channel is *The Notebook*. "Go figure," he says and immediately changes the channel. Mindlessly sifting through channels, he finds *My Dog Skip* and capitulates to it.

Saturday morning Zac wakes to his phone ringing. "Hello," he answers groggily.

"Dude, we still on for tonight?" Adan asks.

"Yeah, I will meet you there around seven. What time is it?"

"Zac, it's noon. Are you still in bed?" Adan laughs.

"Yeah, man, it feels good. I haven't slept this late in years."

"Get up! I got to go. See you tonight."

Zac hangs up and rises from his lost comfort.

The afternoon passes too quickly, and Zac finds himself rushing to get ready. On the way out the door, he looks back at Jake in the egg. "I love you, my boy. I will be back later." He locks the door as he leaves.

Walking along the street in front of the Blue Soul, Zac sees that little Honda with the Border Terrier sticker in the back window. He smiles, thinking about his buddy. As he approaches the car, he notices the driver is still in it, messing with a phone. He continues, wondering what is going on at the Blue Soul tonight. As he passes the car, he looks back over his left shoulder to see who owns it. Multiple waves of emotions overtake him as he sees Mary Ann sitting in the driver's seat. His pace slows as he remembers putting a similar sticker on her truck. He then retraces memories with Jake. He remembers that Jake sat by the driver's door of the car. Now he knows why. Tears swell in his eyes. She has not seen him, so he increases his speed until he enters the Blue Soul while wiping his tears.

Inside he sees Adan by the bar and approaches with his back to the entrance.

"So, Thomas, what's up for tonight?" Adan is asking when Zac arrives.

Thomas points to the stage and says, "You'll see."

They look over to see curtains drawn in front of the stage. "What's that about?" Zac asks, recovering his emotions.

"Give it a half hour. You'll like it. Here, have a couple martinis on me." Thomas hands them the martinis and feverishly starts other cocktails as the growing crowd starts consuming the place.

"Is Derek coming?" Adan asks Zac.

"No. I told him it would not be a good idea."

"Cool. Thanks, Zac."

Zac turns away from the bar and scans the crowd. His face changes as he sees the table closest to the dance floor.

Adan turns to search for available targets and notices the same table. "Dude." Adan places his hand on Zac's shoulder.

"I know." No other words are required as they both recognize Mary Ann and Allison have taken the table.

"Zac is over there with Adan," Allison tells Mary Ann.

"I know. We passed them at the bar when we came in," she says.

"Are you OK with this?"

"Yes, he never did anything wrong. I am all right," she replies as she turns to see Zac and Adan have noticed them. "He looks sad."

"Have you talked with him?" Allison asks.

"Nope."

Allison now remembers that she did not tell Mary Ann about Jake, and now she knows Zac hasn't either. "Um, Mary Ann." Allison's voice quivers.

"Yeah, what?" Mary Ann returns her attention to Allison.

"You have not talked to Zac?"

"No, why?"

"I don't know how to say this. I don't even know if I should."

"What is it? Does Zac have a girlfriend? Did he knock someone up? What?"

"Zac has been sad for a while. Adan told me when we had lunch the day I went to your place for your breakup ice cream. Anyway...Jake died." Allison stares into Mary Ann's eyes.

Mary Ann starts tearing up as she realizes she won't see Jake again. She breaks into tears as she fondly remembers Jake sitting on their chair while she read. She remembers the bite to Zac's butt after he sneaked up on them making love.

"I'm sorry. Adan and I decided Zac should tell you," Allison says as she reaches for Mary Ann.

"It's OK. None of this is your fault. I need you to know that."

"OK," Allison answers.

Mary Ann sits there for a moment. She then rises from her chair, turns directly to Zac, and walks over.

Zac sees her coming and prepares himself.

"Honey," she says as she places a hand on his shoulder.

Zac hasn't heard those emotion-stirring words since she moved out. "Hi," he says softly, looking into her eyes.

"I am so sorry for everything. I didn't know Jake died."

He says nothing as both of their eyes water. He thinks about the car with the sticker, now knowing it is hers. Jake loved her. "I didn't know how or when to tell you," he says apologetically.

She reaches up and places her arms around his neck and hugs him, loving the feel of his arms as he wraps them around her. She kisses his cheek. "You know I love Jake," she says.

"I do. He really loved you, baby."

She starts crying, as does Zac.

Adan, watching this unfold, sits, saddened, silently. Thomas has left the bar and steps out from behind the curtain on the stage. "Folks," he addresses the packed Blue Soul. "I told you I had something special for tonight. So without further delay, I want to introduce you to an old friend of mine. Brian, come out here please."

Mary Ann and Zac, still holding each other, turn their heads, looking over to the stage.

"Ladies and gentleman, I want to introduce you to Brian."

The guitar legend walks out from behind the curtain with his hollow-body electric guitar slung across him as the crowd responds with applause.

"He and his band will be playing tonight, here, live at the Blue Soul," Thomas yells. The curtains are pulled, revealing the band. The familiar strumming of "Stray Cat Strut" starts as the crowd erupts in excitement and commotion as people seek dance partners.

Mary Ann looks up to Zac. "Would you like to dance?" she asks, wiping Zac's tears, then hers.

"I would," he whispers in her ear.

She takes his hand and leads him to the floor. Many patrons are dancing when they start. They begin a slower Lindy Hop due to the pace of the song, uncaring of the others around them. Both saddened as they begin to dance, the chemistry they had begins to show itself as their dancing takes on a life itself, growing to perfection. Zac leads, and she allows him to. Both eyes are still watering from the sadness of Jake's death, yet this emotion is bringing out emotional dancing that is becoming noticeable to everyone in the bar.

Thomas, back at the bar, notices Zac and Mary Ann dancing with love and emotion.

Adan sits and watches the two, noticing the lack of smiles on their faces. As he peers, he understands this is not about the dance. The spins, the steps—everything is perfect.

Allison rises from her chair and moves to the bar next to Adan, saying nothing, just wondering if everyone else sees what they see.

The song continues. The perfection between Zac and Mary Ann does also. Other pairs start to see what's going on and slow their pace, watching Zac and Mary Ann. Oblivious to all except themselves, they continue as they started, alone with each other. The song ends as Zac dips Mary Ann. A spectacular dip, completed to perfection.

Completely arched backward, with watery eyes, Mary Ann notices the rose petals in the floor. Silence envelopes the Blue Soul as even the band recognize something special just happened.

Zac lifts her body to him, face-to-face, embracing her. He finds she is crying, as she finds he is. The moment freezes within the dim lights of the Blue Soul, and tears slowly stream their faces. The crowd slowly begins its applause. Zac and Mary Ann lock eyes. No one else is in their world. Zac thinks to himself, I wonder what Jake would say about this? Is this what Jake was saying?

"finally."